The Learning Works

Mystery and Suspense

Language Arts & Reading Activities

Grades 5–8

Cover Art by Taylor Bruce

Written by Judith B. Steffens and Judy F. Carr • Illustrated by Bev Armstrong

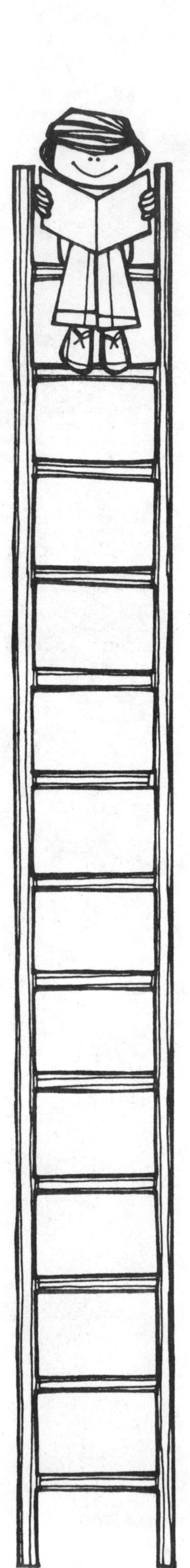

The Learning Works

Edited by Sherri René Butterfield

Contents

Contents
(continued)

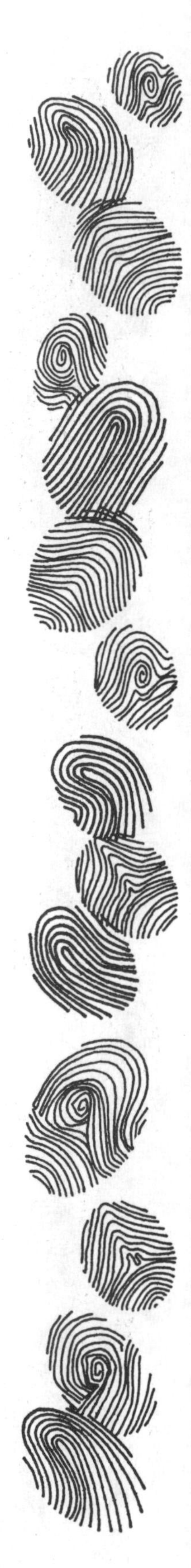

To the Teacher

Mystery and Suspense is a skill-oriented, thematic language arts unit with great appeal for adolescents. It casts individual and group reading skill lessons in a framework of suspense, horror, and creative imagination.

Mystery and Suspense is divided into five sections: Detective Stories, The Mind of the Criminal, Horror and Imagination, Vocabulary, and Skill Stretchers.

Detective Stories includes skill lessons and activities covering sequencing and plot, main idea, supporting details, locating information, foreshadowing, cause and effect, fact or opinion, compare and contrast, drawing conclusions, making inferences, climax, and antagonist/protagonist—all skills that lend themselves easily to detective literature.

The Mind of the Criminal includes skill lessons and activities covering characterization, conflict, flashback, author's purpose, point of view, and tone.

Horror and Imagination includes skill lessons covering setting, characterization, mood, figurative language, and symbol.

Vocabulary includes skill lessons and activities covering context clues, multiple meanings, prefixes, suffixes, dictionary and thesaurus skills, synonyms, antonyms, connotation and denotation, and analogies.

Skill Stretchers includes imaginative formats for student book reports and clever ideas for code, game, puzzle, dramatization, pantomime, and creative writing activities designed to reinforce or enrich the reading and language arts skills taught throughout the unit. You may wish to mount or laminate these pages and keep them together as a classroom resource.

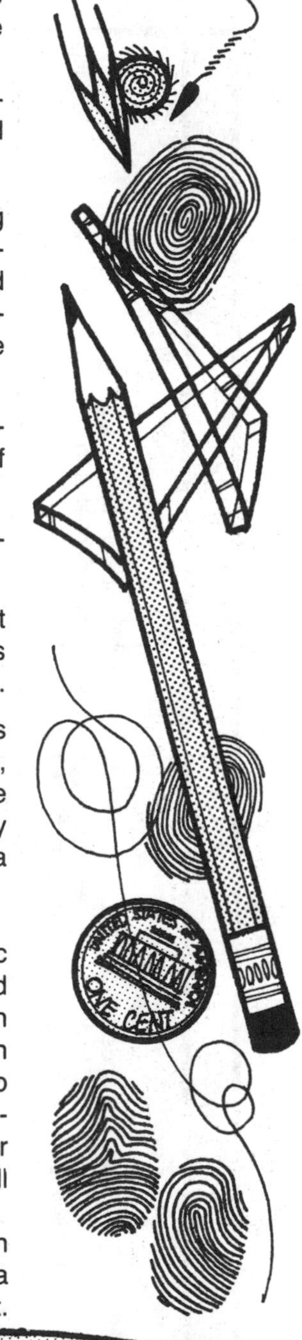

You may use these activities in the order presented or select specific ones to match your students' diagnosed skill development needs. To aid you in making such selections, each activity has been identified by both skill and title in the table of contents. A boxed explanation or definition with examples is provided for each term or concept introduced. Also provided are a bibliography of mystery and suspense literature appropriate for junior and senior high students, a pretest and a posttest for measuring student progress, and an answer key for the tests and for all activities that are not open-ended.

Mystery and Suspense may be used as an independent unit for both homogeneous or heterogeneous classes, as an enrichment unit, as a source of individual skill lessons, or as a supplement to any basal text.

Using This Book

The individual and group activities described in this book can be used in many ways.

	Day 1	Day 2	Day 3	Day 4	Day 5
Homogeneous Group	Group activity to introduce skill Assign story to class to be finished as homework.	Individual skill sheet Review individual skill sheet. Check understanding and application of the concept, term, or skill.	Vocabulary—either a general lesson or a lesson related to the story read Record vocabulary in notebook. Review and collect skill sheets.	Follow-up skill lesson directly related to story Review skill lesson with class. Collect, correct, and save skill lesson.	Enrichment Day Independent novel reading *or* Individual activity sheet *or* Group activity
Heterogeneous Group	Group activity to introduce skill Either assign three levels of the same story or three different stories of differing reading levels to be finished as homework.	Individual skill lesson for entire class Confer with Group A to discuss story while Groups B and C complete skill lesson and begin vocabulary work.	Confer with Group B while Group C completes vocabulary work. Confer with Group C while Groups A and B complete vocabulary work.	Follow-up lesson directly related to story Use one lesson applicable to all three stories or create a separate follow-up lesson for each story (see Sample Inference Lesson on page 35).	Enrichment Day Story sharing *or* Independent novel reading *or* Individual activity sheet *or* Group activity
Basal Reader	Use individual skill sheet and group activity ideas to introduce and reinforce skills found in the reading assignments.				
Notes	**1.** Assign an independent novel as part of each reading unit. **2.** Give quizzes as needed to hold student interest and check progress. **3.** Use individual activity sheets for optional enrichment or as required assignments. **4.** Use the Reading Skills Checklist on page 106 to keep a record of the reading skills students have mastered and those that need additional reinforcement.				

Name ____________________

Pretest

Read the excerpt below.

With a resigned look in her eye, Lindsey trudged down the steep, stone steps of the prison and began to walk toward the parking lot. What a day! Sighing, she turned and looked back. The gray walls of the prison loomed in stark relief against the bright blue sky, the barred windows looking for all the world like animal cages encased in cement. And that, she thought, is just what they are—cages to hold men and women who soon become animals. She thought back, reluctantly, to the man she'd just left, Jake Jones, who was serving the last year of an eight-year stretch for armed robbery—a man without hope. In the time Lindsey had worked with him, she had come to know him well. He could learn, but he wouldn't, and no amount of prodding or effort on her part was going to change that.

Funny how it had all seemed so different to her three months ago. She had arrived on a sunny day, just like today, but optimistic and determined—a literacy volunteer filled with a smug confidence that she could make a difference to these prisoners, a real contribution. Hah! Lindsey flung down her clipboard and books in disgust at her own naïveté. Today had shown her just how wrong she had been. After three months of agonizing, fruitless effort, Jake Jones had ordered her out of his cell. He was through, he'd said. What'd he need to learn to read and write for anyhow? Who was ever gonna give him, a jailbird, a legit job? He musta been nuts when he'd agreed to try.

Well, that was that. Lindsey stooped to pick up the materials she had dropped and headed toward the parking lot. It was then that she heard the warden's voice. She turned and was amazed to see him racing toward her.

Name ______________________

Pretest
(continued)

Read each question below. Then write the correct answer on the numbered line.

1.	Who is the main character in the story?	1.	______________________
2.	From what point of view is the story told?	2.	______________________
3.	What is the setting of the story?	3.	______________________
4.	This passage contains a flashback. If you numbered the story events in the order in which they actually occurred, which event would come first?.	4.	______________________ ______________________
5.	Which event would come last?	5.	______________________
6.	What words are used to introduce the flashback?	6.	______________________ ______________________
7.	What one word would you use to describe the mood the author creates in these opening paragraphs?	7.	______________________
8.	Does she create the mood through setting, situation, or description?	8.	______________________
9.	What words in the first sentence signal this mood?	9.	______________________ ______________________
10.	What kind of conflict did you find in this excerpt?	10.	______________________
11.	What words foreshadow a coming change in mood or action?	11.	______________________ ______________________
12-13.	Compare Lindsey's day today and with her day three months ago. In what two ways are they similar?	12. 13.	______________________ ______________________
14-15.	In what two ways are they different?	14. 15.	______________________ ______________________
16.	The excerpt contains an example of figurative language. What is it?	16.	______________________ ______________________
17.	What do the books and clipboard symbolize for Lindsey?	17.	______________________ ______________________
18.	Is the following a statement of fact or opinion? *This story is fifteen pages long.*	18.	______________________

Name ______________________

Pretest
(continued)

19. What caused Jake Jones to give up? | **19.** ______________________

20. What effect did Jones's decision have on Lindsey? | **20.** ______________________

21-23. The author uses three techniques of characterization to develop the main character. What are they?

21. ______________________

22. ______________________

23. ______________________

24. Why, do you think, did Lindsey become a literacy volunteer in the first place? | **24.** ______________________

25. Is Lindsey angry at Jake for his decision? How do you know? | **25.** ______________________

26. Complete the following analogy.

A gun is to a detective as a ______ is to a porcupine.

26. ______________________

27-28. Write a synonym and an antonym for the word thorough.

27. ***Synonym:*** ______________________

28. ***Antonym:*** ______________________

29. The word dense may mean compact. It may also mean ______. | **29.** ______________________

30. Add a root or base word to the suffix -ology. | **30.** ______________________

31. What does the word you wrote on Line 30 mean? | **31.** ______________________

32. In the word telepathy, what does the prefix tele- mean? | **32.** ______________________

33. What kind of context clue is given in the following sentence?

His poor attitude only exacerbated, or increased, the problem.

33. ______________________

34. What is the denotation of the word mansion? | **34.** ______________________

35. What does the word mansion connote? | **35.** ______________________

Name ______________________________

A Bungled Burglary

> The **Plot** is the sequence of events in the story. **Sequencing** means putting events in chronological order—the order in which they happened.

"Wake up. Wake up, George," urged a frantic Mrs. Thurston as she shook the shoulder of her unconscious husband.

"Ugh...," he groaned softly as his eyes fluttered open. "Where am I?"

"You're in our room at home, George. Don't you remember? Two burglars came in through the sliding door. They crept down the hall and tried to open our bedroom door. The creaking of the bedroom door must have awakened you. You yelled, leaped out of the bed, and went charging after them down the hall. You remember, you bumped into Great-Grandma Sally's old rocker. It's definitely going to need repair! When you got back on your feet, you dashed over to the burglars, and one of them must have hit you on the head with his gun. Before you passed out, you shouted to me to call the police."

"Where are the burglars now?" asked George.

"They must have fled when they realized there were other people in the house. Luckily, you didn't give them time to steal anything. Thank goodness you're okay," replied his wife.

"I'm a hero," muttered George in amazement. "It's a good thing I didn't realize they had a gun when I first chased them. I was sure it was just a flashlight when I saw the gleam. Good grief!" And, once again, George passed out.

List the events from this story in the order in which they happened.

1. ______________________________
2. ______________________________
3. ______________________________
4. ______________________________
5. ______________________________
6. ______________________________
7. ______________________________
8. ______________________________
9. ______________________________
10. ______________________________
11. ______________________________
12. ______________________________
13. ______________________________

Teamwork Detective

Try this and watch class members learn to work together. Presented with many random statements about a crime, students must listen and cooperate to sort information sequentially, draw conclusions, and uncover the solution.

Materials Needed

Teamwork Detective Clue Cards on page 12

Instructions

Before Class

1. Cut apart the clue cards. For extra durability, glue them to tagboard or index cards.
2. Arrange students' desks in a large circle.

During Class

1. Distribute the cards face down, one to each student. Tell students *not* to look at their cards. (Cards should remain face down until the class is told to begin.)
2. Explain that information about a fictitious crime is printed on each of the cards. The goal is to reconstruct the crime, naming the murderer, the weapon, and the motive. Students are to arrange information and events in chronological order. Class members must remain seated and prevent other members from seeing their cards. All information is to be shared orally.
3. Tell students to look at their cards and begin.
4. Make note of the steps the group uses to organize itself and the information. Do *not* help in any way.
5. When the class has finished, ask someone to state, in correct sequential order, the events that occurred on the night in question. Have the class recap the solution process, discussing where they bogged down and how they could have organized themselves and exchanged information more effectively.

Follow-up

Substitute your own clue cards. Any "crime" will work. Be sure to include enough information so that the problem is solvable. For advanced groups, a few red herrings may be included to make the process more challenging.

Teamwork Detective Clue Cards

Florence Floogle, landlady, discovered the body of a young woman in the third floor rear apartment at 8:15 a.m. on March 3.	The police received the call from Mrs. Floogle at 9:00 a.m.
The medical examiner stated that the victim had died between 3:00 and 5:00 a.m. on March 3.	Mr. and Mrs. Smythe opposed the marriage.
Miss Able admitted, under questioning, that she was in love with Mr. Ready.	Miss Able is an unemployed magician's assistant.
A passing patrolman saw John Ready leaving the apartment house at 2:15 a.m. on March 3.	Mrs. Floogle is known to have dizzy spells and has blacked out in the past.
Florence said no one entered or left the apartment house after she locked the front door for the night at midnight.	The weapon, a palette knife, had been wiped clean of prints and left beside the body.
Mr. and Mrs. Elwyn Smythe identified the victim as their only daughter, Abigail, age twenty.	Mr. Ready returned during the evening of March 3. He was obviously distressed to find the police in his apartment. He denied having returned to the apartment before then.
John Ready, an impoverished artist, was engaged to marry Miss Smythe. The wedding date had not been set.	Mrs. Floogle reported numerous verbal battles between Miss Smythe and Miss Able.
Miss Smythe would be independently wealthy after her twenty-first birthday, when she would inherit a large trust fund.	Mr. Ready was carrying a bouquet of flowers and a bottle of wine when he returned to the apartment.
The body was found in the apartment of John Ready.	Mrs. Floogle's apartment is located directly opposite the front entrance. There is no other entrance to the building.
Ruth Able, a tenant in the second floor apartment below Mr. Ready's, said that she heard a violent argument overhead at approximately 1:30 a.m., March 3.	The victim had been stabbed several times; there was evidence of a struggle.

Suspense Storyboards

Everyone loves a cartoon, particularly students. In this activity, students select the eight most important events from stories they read and create a cartoon for each event. An organizational scheme must be developed before any writing or drawing begins.

Materials Needed

pencils
sheets of lined paper
sheets of unlined white paper 18 inches wide
rulers
crayons or marking pens of various colors

Directions

Before Class

1. All students read a mystery, short story, or novel.
2. The teacher makes available needed materials.

During Class

1. On lined paper, each student jots down, in chronological order, the eight key events from the story he or she has read.
2. Using a ruler, each student divides a piece of unlined white paper into nine boxes of equal size.
3. In the first box, the student writes the story title.
4. In each of the other eight boxes, the student writes one sentence describing an important event in the story.
5. Next, the student illustrates each sentence or event. Lack of artistic talent is no problem. Stick figures work just fine.

Follow-up

Create a Suspense Storyboard bulletin board. In the center, put the word **plot** and a definition. Surround this with the students' suspense storyboards.

or

Categorize the storyboards by genre, such as Detective, Mystery, Horror.

Telegram Telepathy

Dangerous Dan is planning a crime that is very similar to the one described in a story you have read. Give him the benefit of your experience. Send him a telegram in which you describe the main ideas of the story.

Remember, telegrams are very expensive—$14.70 for fifteen words or less and 29¢ for each additional word. You may spend no more than $17.60. Make every word count.

TIMELY TELEGRAMS, INC.

TO: ____________________________________

____

____

____

FROM: ____________________________________

Cut-up Caper

HELP! This newspaper account of a robbery was found in shreds in an abandoned house and may be a vital piece of evidence. Can you fill in the supporting details that have been cut from the article? On a separate sheet of paper, write the complete newspaper account, putting all of the events in correct order and inserting the missing details.

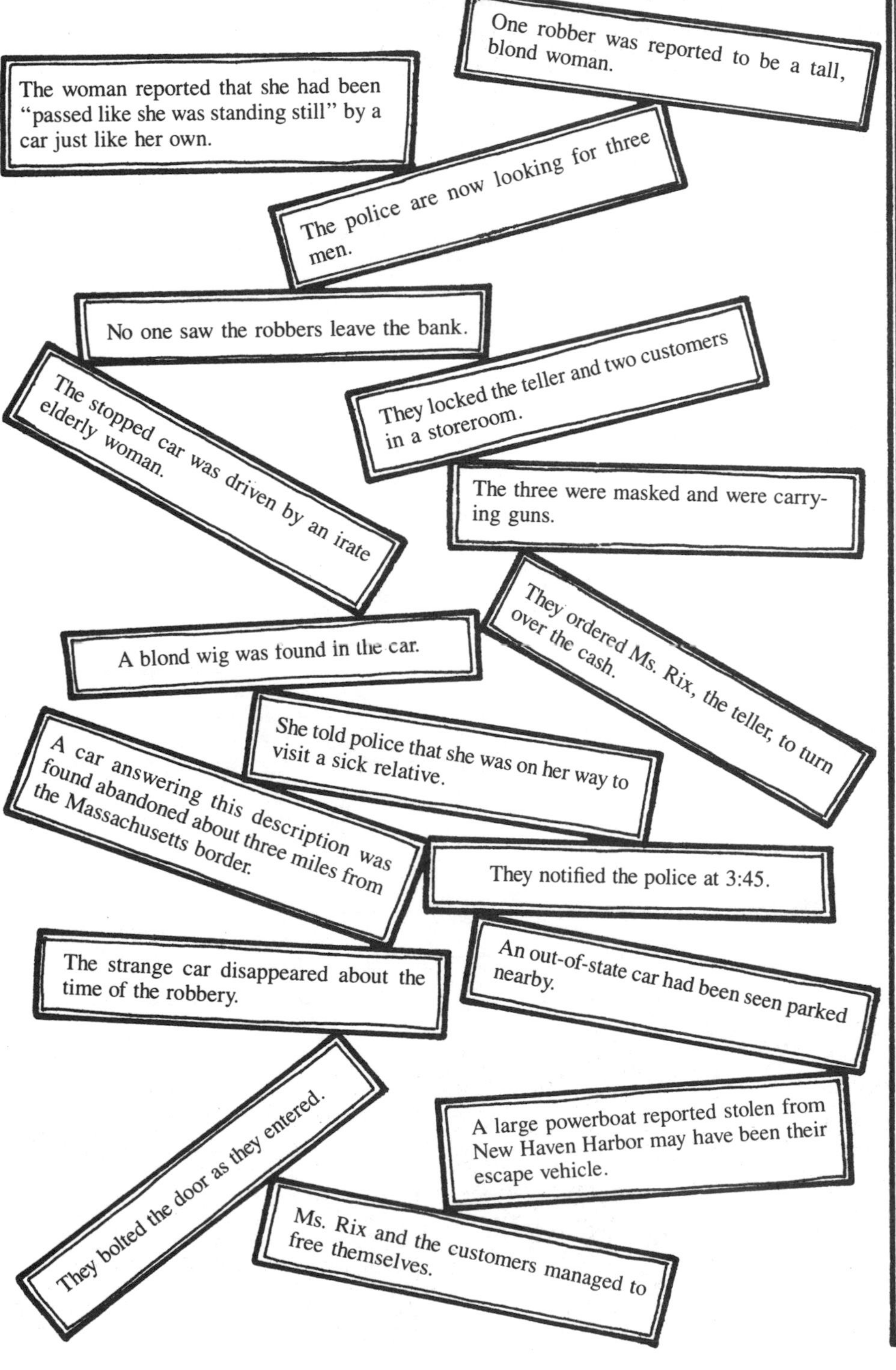

One robber was reported to be a tall, blond woman.

The woman reported that she had been "passed like she was standing still" by a car just like her own.

The police are now looking for three men.

No one saw the robbers leave the bank.

They locked the teller and two customers in a storeroom.

The stopped car was driven by an irate elderly woman.

The three were masked and were carrying guns.

They ordered Ms. Rix, the teller, to turn over the cash.

A blond wig was found in the car.

She told police that she was on her way to visit a sick relative.

A car answering this description was found abandoned about three miles from the Massachusetts border.

They notified the police at 3:45.

The strange car disappeared about the time of the robbery.

An out-of-state car had been seen parked nearby.

A large powerboat reported stolen from New Haven Harbor may have been their escape vehicle.

They bolted the door as they entered.

Ms. Rix and the customers managed to free themselves.

Robbers' Escape Baffles Police

Essex police are reported baffled by the robbery of a local bank late yesterday. Three robbers apparently entered the Essex National Bank at 3:05 p.m.

The robbers were able to leave the bank unhampered at 3:32.

The supposed getaway car was next seen on Route 91, where it was stopped by Massachusetts police.

The robbers are believed to have made a clean getaway.

Anyone with information about this crime is asked to contact the Vermont police.

Real-Life Rogues

Real life is filled with a variety of rogues, persons who have distinguished themselves through their criminal activities. Research the life of one villain from the list on page 104 or from some other source and fill in this stat sheet.

NAME: ____________________

NATIONALITY: ____________________

DATE OF BIRTH: ____________________

DATE OF DEATH: ____________________

PHYSICAL DESCRIPTION: ____________________

PERSONALITY TRAITS (LIST THREE): ____________________

EARLY LIFE: ____________________

CRIMINAL ACTIVITIES: ____________________

IDENTIFYING CHARACTERISTICS OF CRIMES: ____________________

APPREHENDED? YES_____ **NO**_____

IF YES, WHEN AND BY WHOM? ____________________

RECORDER'S NAME: ____________________

Super Sleuth Scroll

Mystery lovers everywhere delight in reading about clever detectives created by superior authors. The amazing feats of some real-life investigators are too often overlooked. Choose a super sleuth from the list on page 104 or from some other source, do a little research, and then complete the scroll that you will award to your private eye at this year's Sleuth Society Supper.

Name ____________________

Find the Foreshadowing

Foreshadowing is giving an indication or warning of what is to come so that the reader can anticipate the mood or action.

Read the passages below.

I. Timothy Johns sighed to himself as he unlocked the door to his office. The chipped lettering on the cracked glass pane was a good indication of how well his private investigation service was doing. He went inside and settled himself in his chair, ruefully eyeing the bills stacked on the corner of the desk. With a determined expression, he began to go through them.

He worked in silence for some time. When he finally finished, he leaned back and was startled to see a middle-aged woman standing in front of him. She wore a well-tailored suit and neat leather gloves. "Well," Tim thought, "things are definitely looking up!"

What words foreshadow a change? Underline them. Do you think things will improve or worsen? Why?

II. The morning had seemed normal enough. The sun was shining, birds were singing, and dew glistened on the short-cropped grass.

What one word suggests something is about to happen? Circle it.

III. Now you try. In the box below, write a foreshadowing clue of your own for the following passage. Then draw an arrow to show its place in the paragraph.

Jenny walked toward the house, humming to herself. She could feel the weight of her pack pressing against her back. She was pleased she had finally reached "civilization" again. Looking about, she began to climb the stairs to the house.

IV. A well-written mystery or detective story always contains information to help you anticipate what will happen, or even to help you solve the crime.

Using a story you have read in class, list four words, phrases, or clauses that the author used to warn you about what was coming.

1. ____________________

2. ____________________

3. ____________________

4. ____________________

Name ______________________________

Expect an Effect

The **effect** is what happened as a result of something; the **cause** is the reason for what happened.
For example: He had been threatened, so he purchased a gun.
What happened? He purchased a gun.
What was the reason? He had been threatened.

A good detective knows there is a reason for everything that happens. Part of solving a mystery depends on knowing *what* happened and *why* it happened.

I. Read each cause-and-effect sentence below. Underline the **effect** (what happened) and circle the **cause** (the reason for what happened). The first one is done for you.

1. Hector had to find a place to hide because (the police were looking for him.)
2. He had robbed the bank because he was desperate for money.
3. Because Hector had left fingerprints on the front door of the bank, the police knew he was the criminal.
4. They would be able to recognize him because he had forgotten to wear a disguise.
5. Because he was frightened, Hector made some stupid mistakes.
6. He ran to his home because he could not think of anywhere else to go.
7. The police were sure to check his home because they had it staked out.
8. Hector burned the money in the fireplace to destroy the evidence.
9. To remember the event, however, he kept one bill.
10. Because he was so foolish, the police were able to charge him with the crime.

Name ______________________________

Expect an Effect
(continued)

II. Match the **effects** with their **causes** by writing the correct letter on each line.

Effect

___ **1.** The defendant was on trial

___ **2.** The lawyer defended his client

___ **3.** The judge pounded the bench with his gavel

___ **4.** The newspaper reporters took notes

___ **5.** The prosecutor brought charges against the defendant

Cause

A. because there was too much noise in the courtroom.
B. because he believed the woman was innocent.
C. because he believed the woman was guilty.
D. because they were supposed to write stories about the trial.
E. because she was accused of stealing the money.

III. Match the **causes** with their **effects** by writing the correct letter on each line.

Cause

___ **1.** because he wanted to see what was making the strange noise.

___ **2.** because he was afraid to close his eyes.

___ **3.** because he saw a bear staring at him.

___ **4.** so that he could see better.

___ **5.** because he thought he heard a strange noise outside his window.

Effect

A. John Meyers could not go to sleep
B. He listened very carefully
C. John looked out the window
D. He turned on a flashlight
E. John screamed

Sequence Review: For bonus points, write the five cause-and-effect events listed in Section III in sequence on the lines below.

1. ______________________________

____

2. ______________________________

____

3. ______________________________

____

4. ______________________________

____

5. ______________________________

____

Now, pretend that you are an ace reporter. On a separate sheet of paper, write a newspaper article based on these five events. Feel free to enliven your account with additional vivid detail.

And What Happened Next?

Students race against the clock to develop logically the character and situation introduced to them by the teacher.

Materials Needed

a timer, preferably one that rings when the time is up
a description of a character in a situation

Instructions

Before Class

1. Locate a timer to use for this activity.
2. Become familiar with the character and situation described below.

During Class

1. Have students sit in a circle.
2. Tell students they are going to create a series of cause-and-effect events for the character and situation given them. After each event is described, the whole class says, "And then . . . ," before the next student adds his portion. Each episode must follow logically and be consistent with the character developed by the teacher. No one can bring the story to a close until the timer goes off, at which time the *next* student must finish the story.
3. Start the story.

   Now that Jeremy had the loot hidden, he was anxious to get out of the forest, head home, and make plans for his day's "earnings." Aware that a light rain was starting to fall, he searched frantically for a familiar path. Suddenly, a bolt of lightning hit a tree not a hundred feet from where he stood. Now truly frightened, Jeremy realized that he was hopelessly lost.

4. Set the timer for ten minutes.
5. Monitor the activity to be sure that each episode follows logically.

Follow-up

Have students create other characters in situations to use during this activity.

Name ______________________

Factual Facts and Obvious Opinions

A **fact** is a statement that has been or can be proved to be true.
Example: The burglar robbed two banks last month.
An **opinion** is a statement that is believed but cannot be proved.
Example: All burglars like to rob banks.

Attention all mystery lovers! Here's a tip that's sure to sharpen your powers of deduction. When questioning a witness, a detective must understand the difference between a fact and an opinion. Read each statement below. Write an **F** on the line if the statement is a **fact**. Write an **O** on the line if the statement is an **opinion**.

___ **1.** Edgar Allan Poe was born in Boston in 1809.
___ **2.** He attended the U.S. Military Academy at West Point, New York.
___ **3.** Poe wrote during the 1830s and 1840s.
___ **4.** Poe was an excellent writer.
___ **5.** He wrote poems and short stories.
___ **6.** Poe won a short-story competition in 1833.
___ **7.** One of Poe's most famous short stories is "The Murders in the Rue Morgue."
___ **8.** "The Murders in the Rue Morgue" was the first detective story ever written.
___ **9.** In "The Murders in the Rue Morgue," Poe introduced the literary detective C. Auguste Dupin.
___ **10.** Poe also wrote short stories called "The Telltale Heart" and "The Fall of the House of Usher."
___ **11.** Poe's tales are often frightening and dreary.
___ **12.** Edgar Allan Poe was one of the world's best writers of mystery and horror.
___ **13.** In Poe's story entitled "The Pit and the Pendulum," the reader is never told what lies in the pit.
___ **14.** In his poem entitled "The Raven," Poe used alliteration and internal rhyme.
___ **15.** Edgar Allan Poe died in 1849.

Name ____________________

Create a Crime

A burglary has just taken place. The only witnesses are Kent C. Wright, vice-president of the Pacific International Bank, and Ida Klare, a housewife and customer of the bank.

What happened? Recreate the crime by recording statements of fact and opinion made to the police by the two witnesses. Include five statements of fact and five of opinion.

Fact

Mr. Wright: ____________________

____

Mrs. Klare: ____________________

____

Mr. Wright: ____________________

____

Mrs. Klare: ____________________

____

Mr. Wright: ____________________

____

Opinion

Mrs. Klare: ____________________

____

Mr. Wright: ____________________

____

Mrs. Klare: ____________________

____

Mr. Wright: ____________________

____

Mrs. Klare: ____________________

____

Fact or Feeling?

Try a little friendly competition while you reinforce a skill. To win this relay game, students must be able to distinguish fact from feeling, or opinion.

Materials Needed

None

Instructions

Before Class

Have students read a story with a mystery and suspense theme.

During Class

1. Divide the class into two teams, A and B.
2. Instruct the class that this is a fact-or-opinion relay. The first person on Team A states a fact about the story read. Then the first person on Team B states an opinion on the same topic. Next, the second person on Team B states a second fact from the story. The second person on Team A states an opinion about the fact.
3. Keep score on the chalkboard. A point is earned each time a fact or an opinion is stated correctly.

Follow-up

Tell each student to find a news story about a crime. Have students read their stories carefully and underline the facts they contain in blue and the opinions they contain in red. Discuss the essential differences between a news story and an editorial. Explain that news stories should consist primarily of facts; opinions included within these stories should appear in quotation marks and be attributed to a source.

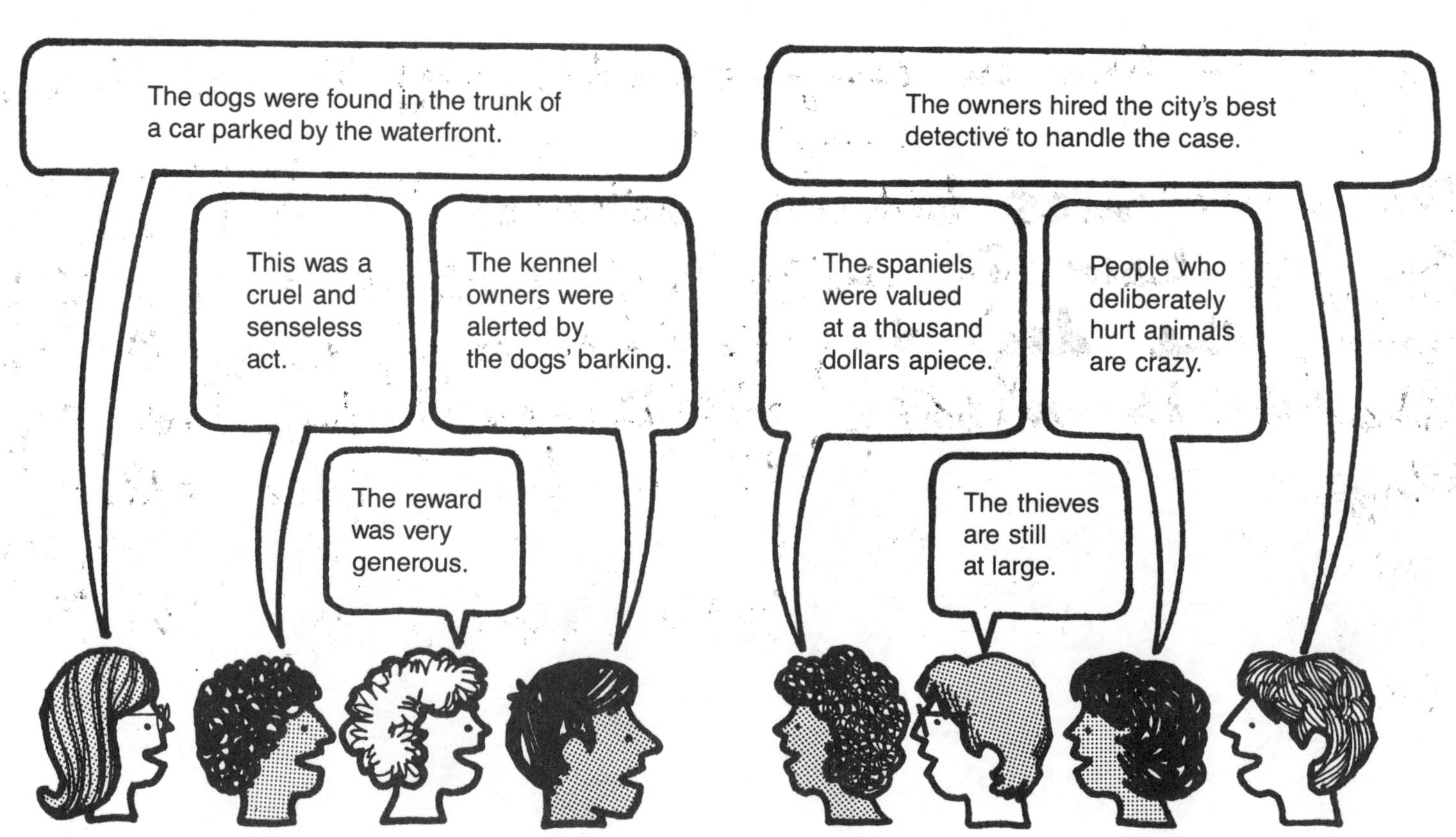

Name ______________________

Detail Detective

To **compare** is to show the ways in which similar things are alike or different. To **contrast** is to show the ways in which unlike things are different.

Pictures A and B are similar but not identical. They are alike in some ways and different in other ways. You be the detective. Look closely at the details. **Compare** these two pictures by finding some of the similarities and differences between them. On the lines below, list two ways in which these pictures differ and two ways in which they are alike.

A

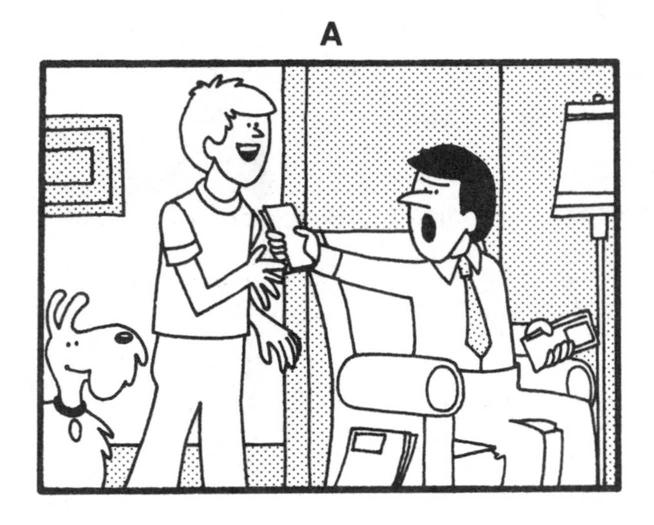

B

Differences

1. The ______________ is missing in Picture B.

2. ____

____

Similarities

1. Both pictures show ______________________________

____

2. ____

____

The facial expressions of the boy and the man in Picture A are quite different. On the lines below, write two sentences in which you **contrast** these facial expressions.

1. ____

____

2. ____

____

Name ____________________

Proctor City Problem

Pat Palmer is a policeman who has been in the Proctor City Police Department for twenty years. His current assignment is to track down Tony the Thug, an eighteen-year-old thief who is alleged to have robbed Sonny's Service Station. Look at the character traits named on the badge. On the lines below each man's name, list the traits that might be used to describe him. Some of the traits may be used to describe both men.

P. C. P. D.

kind	**short-tempered**	**neat**
greedy	**middle-aged**	**single**
young	**power-hungry**	**honest**
dishonest	**trustworthy**	**stubborn**
patient	**emotional**	**thorough**
male	**dangerous**	**cold**

Pat the Policeman

____
____
____
____
____
____

Tony the Thug

____
____
____
____
____
____

Using words from the lists above, write two sentences in which you **contrast** these two very different men.

1. ____________________
____

2. ____________________
____

Tune in Tomorrow

Watch students learn to draw conclusions as they discuss each new episode of "The Case of the Unlucky Victim."
1. Cut episodes apart along the dotted lines.
2. Either duplicate each episode or create a transparency.
3. Present students with one episode each day until, at the end of five days, the case is solved.

The Case of the Unlucky Victim
Episode One

The corpse of Jim Seward was lying face down on the floor of the room, strangely silent in contrast to the noise and activity outside. Blood seeped through his white coat, around the thin handle of a knife that protruded from his left shoulder. In the hall outside, people bustled back and forth, while an intercom blared.

1. *Where did the murder take place?* ____________________

____

____

2. *What clues tell you so?* ____________________

____

____

The Case of the Unlucky Victim
Episode Two

Suddenly the doorknob turned, and Sally Sawyer crept into the room. Small and blonde, she looked nervously about, feeling for the light switch with her right hand. Suddenly light flooded the long, cold room. Sally stood there for a few minutes, unmoving; then she screamed and dashed into the hall.

1. *Is Sally feeling guilty about something? Did she know the corpse was there?* ____________________

____

____

____

2. *What should you remember about Sally?* ____________________

____

Tune in Tomorrow
(continued)

The Case of the Unlucky Victim
Episode Three

In a few minutes, the room was filled with noise and commotion. Lieutenant Joshua Rix stood over the body watching the doctor make his cursory examination. With a sigh, Dr. Jones straightened and announced, "Only been dead a few minutes. Stab wound probably killed him, but I'll know more when I get him down to the lab. At least he waited until I finished my dinner. I can't stand working on an empty stomach."

Feeling queasy, Rix watched the doctor cover the body and signal the attendants to take it away. Suddenly Rix yelled, "Stop!" He bent down and removed a small scrap of paper clutched in the corpse's now-stiffening hand.

1. What evidence suggests the crime was committed recently?

____

____

2. At approximately what time of day was the crime committed?

____

____

The Case of the Unlucky Victim
Episode Four

Eagerly, Rix unfolded the scrap and then sighed in frustration. The paper was bare except for the notation $x/y^3 =$ in the upper right-hand corner. "He's all yours, Doc," he growled in a disgusted way, folding the paper into his notebook. Glumly he watched as the doctor shrugged on a heavy overcoat and stamped out through a rear door, following the corpse on its stretcher.

Puzzled, Rix stalked toward the outer door and threw it open. He beckoned brusquely to the man standing outside. Dr. Sam Small came into the room. Small sighed as he perched himself on one of the tables running the length of the room, a cigarette clutched in his left hand. "My gosh," he said, "it's an awful thing!" Without speaking, Rix handed him the scrap. After another moment of silence, Small said, "Nope, doesn't mean a thing to me. I can't see how that would cause Jim's death. I mean, who would want to stab a man over a scrap of worthless paper?"

1. Does Small know more than he's admitting? How do you know?

____

____

____

2. What further evidence do you have as to the location of the murder?

____

____

Tune in Tomorrow
(continued)

The Case of the Unlucky Victim
Episode Five

Just then Sally Sawyer, pale and shaken, entered the room. She was accompanied by a tall, heavyset man with a determined expression. "Look here," he said, "I won't have Drs. Sawyer and Small disturbed. Their work is very valuable, particularly now with Jim Seward gone. As his assistants, they're the only ones who can continue his work with the fiber. I don't mind telling you this is a big one!"

Lieutenant Rix smiled. "I'm afraid," he said, "that they won't be available too much longer. I'm taking them in for murder."

1. *Are Sawyer and Small in collusion? Why can you make this assumption?*

____

____

2. *Where did the crime take place? How do you know?*

____

____

____

3. *Who committed the actual murder?*

____

____

4. *Who is the determined gentleman with Dr. Sawyer?*

____

____

Name ____________________

Caption This

Drawing conclusions means reaching a decision or making a judgment based on a body of evidence or group of facts.

Being able to draw accurate conclusions is an important skill for any investigator. Test your own ability to draw conclusions with the cartoon below. Look for details that provide clues about what is happening and what is going to happen next.

____________________ ____________________ ____________________ ____________________

____________________ ____________________ ____________________ ____________________

Draw Conclusions

1. In Frame 1, the damsel is screaming because ____________________.
2. In Frame 2, the villain is smiling because ____________________.
3. In Frame 3, the damsel looks ____________________ and is clearly about to ____________________.
4. In Frame 4, the villain has been ____________________, and the story ends happily.

Write Captions

Relying on what you think happened, write an appropriate caption for each cartoon frame. Then fill in missing pictorial details. Make sure that what you add to each drawing is in keeping with the story.

Be the Cartoonist

On a separate sheet of paper, create a four-frame cartoon strip. Omit captions but provide sufficient picture clues so that the reader can easily draw conclusions about what is going on.

Let Your Imagination Go!

In this "sensational" activity, students must first identify a series of sounds and then put those sounds together to create an original radio script.

Instructions

Before Class

Record the following sounds:

- a series of soft footsteps
- someone clearing his throat
- keys rattling against a doorknob
- a creaking door opening
- heavy breathing
- a piece of furniture being knocked over
- breaking glass
- a telephone ringing
- a scream
- running water
- running footsteps
- a slamming door
- a police siren

During Class

1. Play the tape and tell students to list the sounds they hear.
2. Ask students to create an original radio script in which they use these sounds in this same order.

   Example:

   Jill was sitting quietly in the darkness of her apartment, when she heard soft footsteps coming down the hall.

   (Sound Effect 1)

   Sitting absolutely still, Jill tried to convince herself that the steps had gone past her door. Then she heard the soft sound of someone clearing his throat.

   (Sound Effect 2)

3. Check the narrations to be certain students have drawn conclusions about the sounds they heard.
4. Have several students read their narrations while you dub in the sound effects.

Round Table Detective

Armed with only two clues and questions that require yes or no answers, students reconstruct the details of a crime.

Materials Needed

a plot summary

Instructions

Before Class

1. Select a plot summary to use for this activity. A synopsis of any short mystery story or the newspaper account of an actual crime will work well. Here is one example:

   Synopsis: A well-known composer finds himself unable to write—his creativity gone. For some time he has managed to parry the inquiries of his agent and the press, but time is running out. One evening, while sitting despondently in a small coffeehouse, he meets a young woman, a newcomer to the city. She recognizes him instantly and tells him that she has just composed a song and would like his opinion. One glance at the musical score she produces convinces him that the song will be a hit—his hit. On the pretense of looking over other material she has written, he accompanies her back to the room she has rented. Once there, he strangles her and leaves, taking the musical score and any other compositions he can find.

   Clues: a corpse and a small notebook, seemingly empty but containing the faint imprint of several bars of music.

2. Teacher, or person who is designated the leader, reads the plot summary silently.

During Class

1. Students are seated in a circle.
2. The leader presents two clues to the group.
3. Students use judicious questions to reconstruct the crime—the identity of the victim, the perpetrator, the motive, and the means.
4. Students may ask only questions that can be answered with a yes or no by the leader. The leader may respond "not relevant" if the question is not pertinent to the crime. The leader may *not* volunteer additional information of any kind.
5. A student who asks a question that has already been asked is out of the game.

Follow-up

Students each write a synopsis to use in future Round Table Detective sessions.

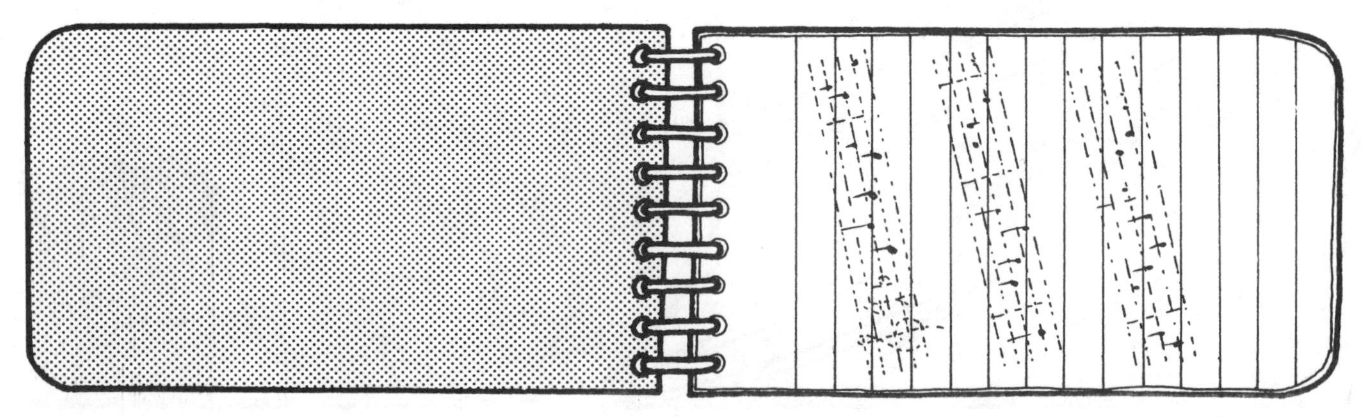

Coat Rack Mystery Guest

Here's a group activity that is guaranteed to meet with positive student response. In this introduction to inferential reading skills, pieces of clothing are added, one at a time, to an old-fashioned coat rack to create an imaginary mystery guest.

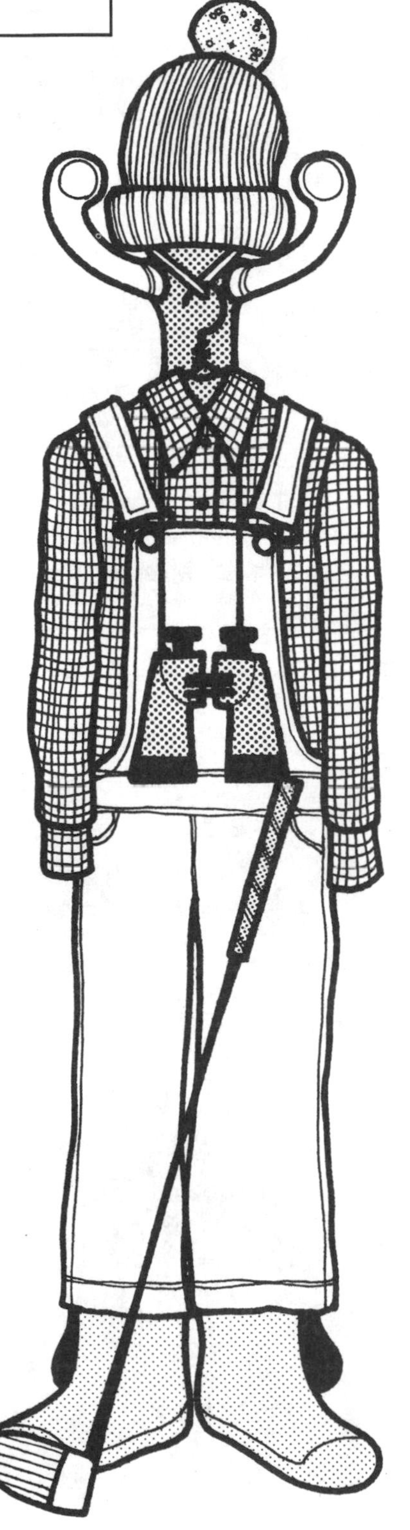

Materials Needed

old-fashioned coat rack
assortment of clothing, headgear, and footwear
props such as a cane, paintbrush, tennis racket

Instructions

Before Class

1. On the day before class, tell the group they will be having a mystery guest the next day.
2. Decide what type of character will be created and gather the appropriate clothing and props.
3. Plan the order in which the items will be placed on the rack. To draw a wide range of responses from the students, keep the figure as ambiguous as possible until the last minute. For example, old slippers, a baggy pair of trousers, and a pipe may suggest a retired gentlemen—until a beret and a paint-spattered shirt are added.
4. Tie trousers and shirt to hangers with strings so that they will hang correctly.

During Class

1. Place the coat rack in front of the room and ask the students to assume that it represents a person with a definite personality. (This may lead to some humorous responses—"Well, he's definitely a person with a few hang-ups.")
2. Place an article of clothing on the rack. Ask the class what statements can now be made about the individual. Ask for evidence to support the statements made. Explain that these educated guesses are called **inferences**.
3. Continue to place items on the rack, each time asking the class to infer something about the guest.
4. At the conclusion of the activity, introduce the guest to the class and review the process of making inferences.

Follow-up

1. Have class members name the guest.
2. Prop the visitor in the corner of the room where he or she can serve as a reminder of the skill that has been introduced.

Name ____________________

Inference Incidents

An **inference** is an educated guess based on facts or premises. In the inference process, reasoning is used to come up with a single judgment based on the evidence available.

I. As the great detective I. M. Smart, you have been presented with three clues: a splinter of wood; a whimpering, maltreated dog; a shredded pair of nylons. You are investigating the case of a missing child. What might you infer if you found these clues in the following settings?

1. a circus ____________________

____

2. a rural countryside ____________________

____

3. an urban highrise ____________________

____

II. The following statements have been taken from a well-known story, "The Splinter," by Mary Roberts Rinehart. What two things can you infer from each?

"Dr. Mitchell limped to the street door and furiously threw it open."

1. ____________________

2. ____________________

"Mrs. Hunt's kitchen was a dreary room, floored with linoleum and with a tin coffee pot on the rusty stove."

1. ____________________

2. ____________________

"Mrs. Hunt's heavy coat had accumulated considerable brush and pine needles, and below it her stockings were torn to rags."

1. ____________________

2. ____________________

Sample Inference Lesson

After the skill has been introduced to the large group and practiced by individuals, it should be reinforced with a worksheet keyed to a story students are reading. Set it up as shown below.

Select six clues from the story.

Review a skill that you have taught previously.

Name ____________

Clues and Conclusions

I. Drawing Conclusions and Making Inferences

Next to each clue, write the conclusion you can draw from it.

A. the pine splinter ____________
B. Wags kept trying to get free. ____________
C. Wags was found near the road to the quarry. ____________
D. Mrs. Hunt got rid of Johnny's things. ____________
E. Mrs. Hunt went looking for Wags with a flashlight. ____________
F. Mrs. Hunt arranged to have her car taken out of storage. ____________

II. Skill Review: Supporting Details

Find two pieces of evidence from the story to support each of the following statements.

A. Pete was a brave boy.
____
____

B. Mrs. Hunt wanted the dog to die.
____
____

C. The dog knew something about Johnny's disappearance.
____
____

D. Mrs. Hunt had a motive for desiring the boy's disappearance.
____
____

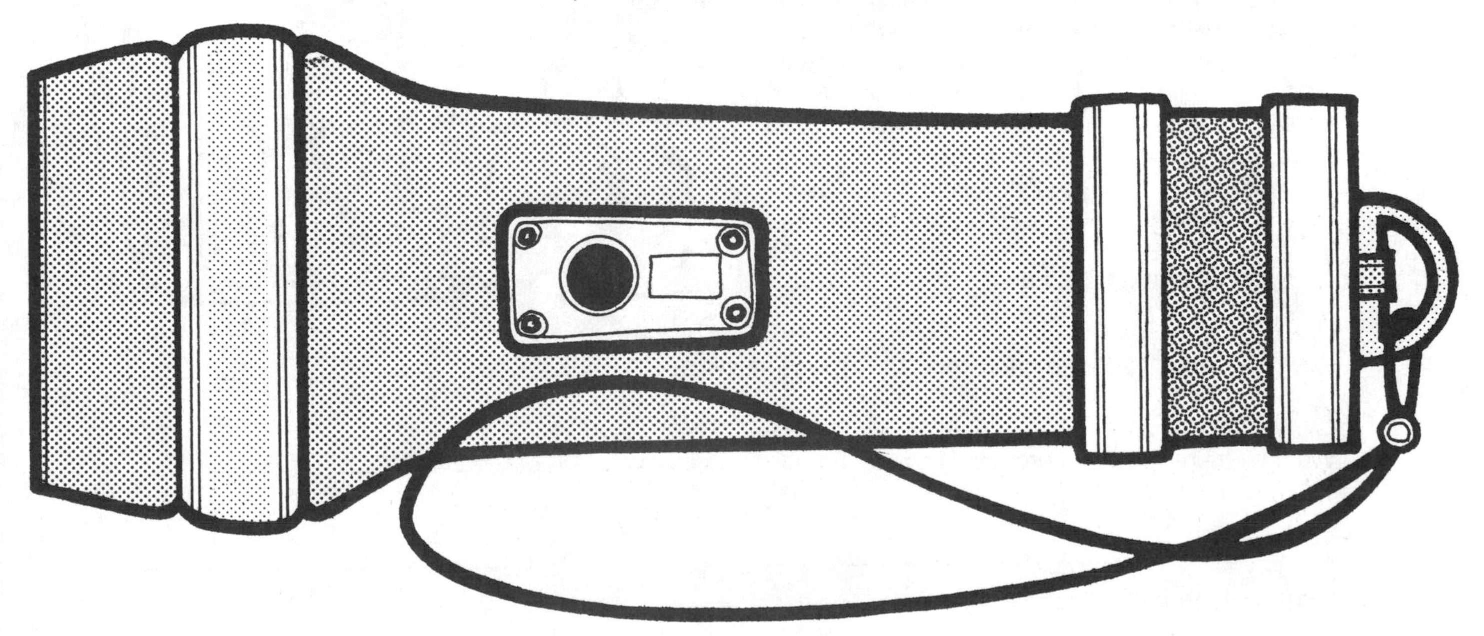

Name ____________________

Quick Crimes

The **climax** of the story is the turning point, the moment at which the conflict is resolved.

The Case of the Affluent Heiress

Detective Alias Smith frowned down at the unkempt young man sitting in front of him. He certainly appeared to be genuinely upset by his wife's death. The body of Sally Bartlett, age thirty-six, had been found some time earlier at the foot of Dead Man's Ravine. Her death had appeared to be the result of an auto accident, but close examination had revealed that Sally's expensive car, with the ignition key in the off position, had been pushed over the cliff. Only minutes ago, the lab had reported that the victim had been drugged before her death. With a sigh, Smith listened to the young man. Bartlett looked tired. He had been awakened a short time ago and told only that his wife had died in an auto accident. He had been accompanied by a police sergeant to the station, where he now sat despondently.

"I'm telling you," he said, "she was a wonderful wife. She was so sensitive to my work. Why, just tonight she insisted I skip the party so that I could work in my studio on a project that's going particularly well. I just couldn't believe it when you called!"

"Hmm," said Detective Smith, "yet your friends report you've been having marital difficulties."

"Never," replied Bartlett. "Those people just spend their time gossiping. Sally and I were meant for each other. I don't know what I'll do without her. She was an inspiration. I just wish she'd used better sense. I warned her not to drive herself home if she drank. That's such a bad stretch of road. I don't know how I'll manage, but somehow I'll have to carry on."

"The only carrying on you'll do," said Alias, "will be in jail. I'm arresting you for the murder of your wife."

Answer the following questions.

1. How did Detective Smith know that Bartlett was guilty? ____________________

____

2. What piece of evidence provided the turning point, or climax, for Detective Smith? ____________________

____

____

Still puzzled? See your teacher for the solution.

Name ____________________

Quick Crime Creation

Puzzle your friends with your own Quick Crime, a brief story in which the reader is presented with a plot summary, all of the evidence, and even the name of the guilty party. Let your friends decide how the detective identified the criminal—if they can!

Here are the steps the author used to create "The Case of the Affluent Heiress." Use them to write your own Quick Crime.

The Case of the Affluent Heiress	Your Own Quick Crime
1. Decide on the crime.	
murder	____________________
2. Decide on the flaw that will reveal the identity of the criminal.	
The murderer couldn't have known where the victim died as he was told only that she had died in a car accident.	____________________ ____________________ ____________________ ____________________
3. Decide on the identity of the characters in the story. Limit yourself to no more than four.	
Sally Bartlett is the victim. Her husband, John Bartlett, is the murderer. Alias Smith is the detective.	____________________ ____________________ ____________________ ____________________
4. Select a motive for the crime.	
Sally is a wealthy heiress, while John is a down-and-out artist. They have had marital problems. The motive is greed.	____________________ ____________________ ____________________ ____________________ ____________________
5. Create a list of events in the crime, up to and including the announcement of the guilty party.	
Sally Bartlett, wealthy heiress, is found in her car at the bottom of Dead Man's Ravine, the apparent victim of an auto accident.	____________________ ____________________ ____________________ ____________________

Name ____________________

Quick Crime Creation
(continued)

The detective returns to the lab where he discovers the victim was drugged before her death.

The police call John Bartlett at his studio. He is awakened with difficulty and explains that he often sleeps at his studio on nights when he has been working late.

Friends report that the couple has had marital difficulties, although neither talked much about their relationship.

John Bartlett arrives at the station and seems genuinely saddened when told that his wife has died in a car crash. He denies marital difficulties.

6. Decide on the climax of the story—the moment at which you will insert the flaw to reveal the criminal and thus provide a turning point for the detective.

When questioned about his wife's death, John becomes flustered and asserts that he had warned her not to drive after partying—particularly on that dangerous section of road.

Alias Smith tells John he is under arrest for his wife's murder.

7. Now write your own Quick Crime. Begin with the moment when the detective is questioning the suspect.

Name ______________________

Television Twosomes

The **protagonist** is the leading character or hero of a story. The **antagonist** is an opponent, the adversary of the protagonist.

Complete this assignment while you watch one of your favorite television programs. Choose any show that involves a number of characters. A detective show would work particularly well. Then answer the questions and fill in the blanks below.

____
(program title)

Who was the protagonist? ______________________

Who was the antagonist? ______________________

Did they look alike or different? ______________________

In what ways? ______________________

____

List two examples that show the protagonist was the hero of this story.

____

____

List two things the antagonist did to oppose the protagonist.

____

____

Who was the winner? ______________________

Why? ______________________

____

ON OFF | VOLUME | HORIZ | VERT | COLOR | BRIGHT | STAR | 3 | CHANNEL HIGH | CHANNEL LOW

Melodrama Merriment

Your class is sure to enjoy presenting these delightful melodramas, complete with villainous villains, distressed damsels, and heroic heroes.

Materials Needed

Melodrama Merriment Cards from page 41
scissors
index cards
tagboard
tape or glue

Instructions

Before Class

1. Cut Melodrama Merriment Cards apart along the dotted lines and mount them on index cards.
2. Prepare three signs, one reading **Boo**, one reading **Hiss**, and one reading **Hooray!**

During Class

1. Explain the **melodrama** to your students.
   - It usually involves stereotyped characters, including a villainous villain dressed in black; a sweet heroine who seems to be incapable of taking any positive action but does a great deal of hand wringing and screaming; and a manly hero, dressed in white, who is always available to rescue the damsel, whatever the situation.
   - Actions and expressions are exaggerated to convey the personalities of the characters to the audience.
   - The action may be accompanied by music and/or title, character, and subtitle cards.
   - It is often staged with a minimum of props.
2. Divide the class into groups of three.
3. Give each group a Melodrama Merriment Card and four or five sheets of construction paper for subtitles.
4. Ask each group to
   - create a story that has a beginning, development, climax, and solution, using the setting, characters, and situation described on the card.
   - dramatize the story and be prepared to present it the following day.
   - create title and subtitle cards for their production.
5. Give class members the rest of the period to prepare their melodramas.

Follow-up

Students present melodramas for another class.

Melodrama Merriment Cards

Setting: a railroad track
Characters: Pernicious Pat
Poor Pearl
Handsome Henry
Situation: Poor Pearl has been tied to the track by Pernicious Pat. He will release her only if she agrees to marry him. Oh, no, a train is approaching!

Setting: on a small boat at sea
Characters: Bad Bartholomew
Marvelous Max
Nora Noswim
Situation: Jaws III circles the boat as Nora Noswim stands on the bow, her arms tied behind her back. Will Nora agree to marry Bad Bartholomew and thus avoid having to learn to swim—rapidly? Or, will Marvelous Max arrive in time to save her from her terrible fate?

Setting: a gloomy cave
Characters: Despicable Dan
Brave Bart
Tantalizing Tilly
Situation: Tilly has just discovered a lost treasure, using a map left her by her recently departed dad. Unfortunately, Despicable Dan has followed her to the cave and is about to steal the fortune. Zounds!

Setting: at the top of a waterfall
Characters: Manly Myron
Delightful Dora
Boris Badheart
Situation: Paralyzed with fear, Dora stands at the top of No-Bottom Falls in the clutches of the evil Boris Badheart. Will Dora reveal the hideout of the marvelous Manly Myron or plunge to her death? But wait, who is that swimming below the falls?

Setting: a sawmill
Characters: Nestor Nogood
Sally Sweetlips
Heroic Harry
Situation: The buzz saw draws nearer to poor Sally's bound body, but villainous Nestor Nogood will not release her unless she agrees to turn over the deed to the family estate. Will Heroic Harry arrive in time?

Setting: a hot-air balloon
Characters: Caustic Carl
Joyous Jane
Gorgeous George
Situation: Alas, poor Jane has been abducted by the evil Caustic Carl. They are now aloft in Carl's hot-air balloon headed for Siberia. Can George reach her in time—or even reach her at all?

Setting: an isolated mountain cabin
Characters: Paula Pureheart
Sterling Stan
Icecold Ira
Situation: Blizzards rage, but it's out into the cold with Paula Pureheart unless she pays the long overdue rent. Will Sterling Stan arrive with the money in time to save Paula from hypothermia?

Setting: at the edge of a cliff
Characters: Belinda Beloved
Dangerous Don
Wonderful William
Situation: Dangerous Don is determined to escape and take poor Belinda with him. Horrors! They've just run out of path and are at the edge of the cliff. If Don can't have her, no one will, he vows. It's a rocky situation. Will Wonderful William wander by before it's too late?

Name ______________________

Character Clues

There are five ways in which you can tell what a character is like. Consider the case of Superstitious Frieda Sylvester.

1. What the character says:

Example: "But, Jason, how can you possibly expect me to go out with you tomorrow night? You know terrible things can happen on Friday the thirteenth."

2. What the character does:

Example: As she progressed up Fiftieth Street, Frieda noticed that a ladder stretched from the curb to an upper window of the Acme Point Building. Window washers were at work. Rather than risk the effects of walking under the ladder, she crossed the street and proceeded on her way.

3. What other characters say about the character:

Example: Jason, to Frieda's mother: "I realize that Frieda has had some unfortunate experiences on Friday the thirteenth, but this is too much. I am not going to let *her* quirks ruin *my* life!"

4. How other characters act toward the character:

Example: After Frieda saw three black cats, Jason automatically handed her the salt shaker so she could throw salt over her shoulder.

5. What the author says about the character:

Example: Frieda's superstitions affected her life drastically, turning even a walk to the store into a challenge.

Use each of these five ways to help your readers learn about Loren Reinhardt, a seven-year-old boy who is afraid of the dark.

1. What the character says: ______________________

____

2. What the character does: ______________________

____

3. What another character says about him: ______________________

____

4. How another character acts toward him: ______________________

____

5. What you, as the author, say about the character: ______________________

____

Name ______________________

Building Character

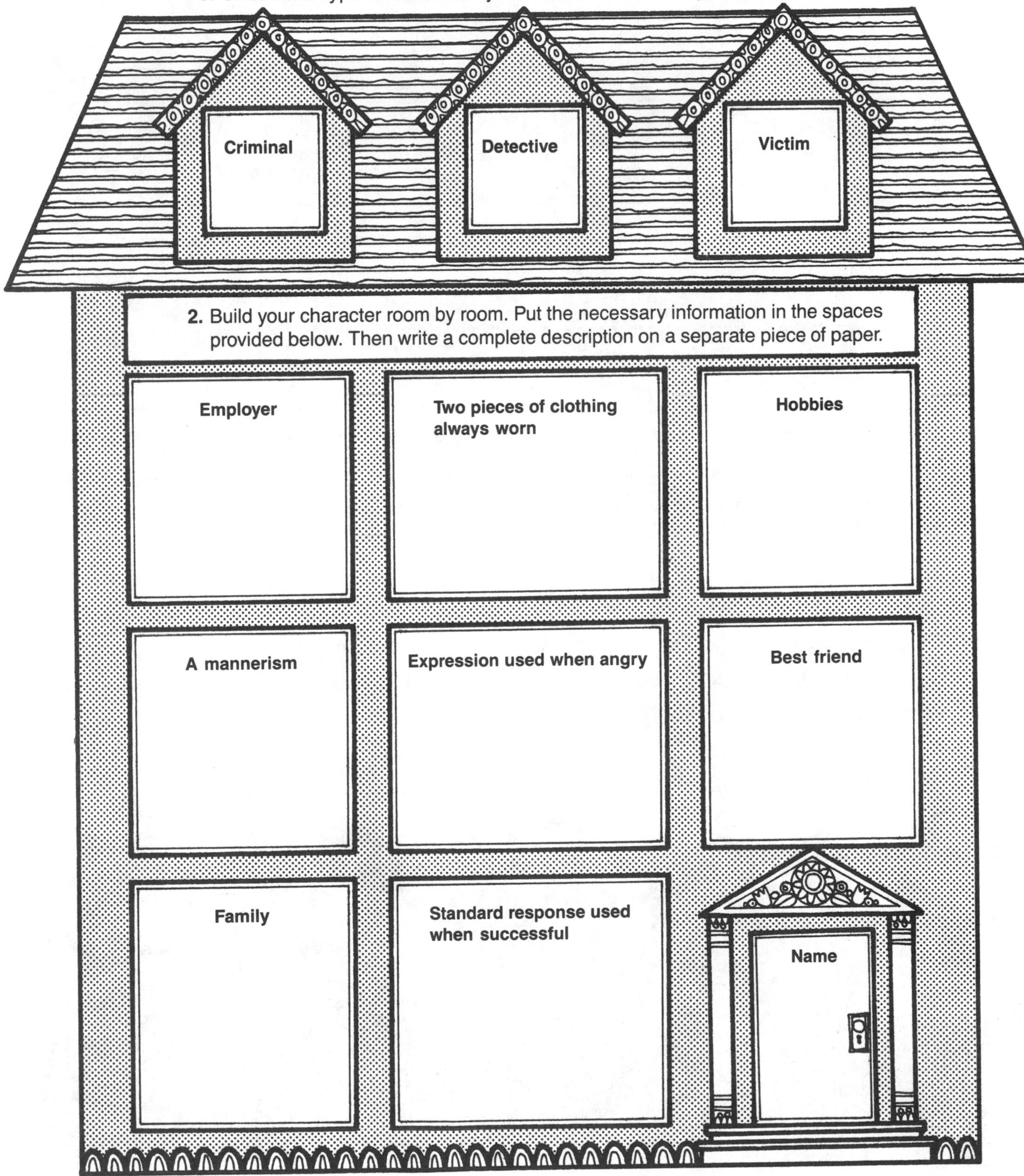

Name ______________________________

Character Clarification

I. How well do you know the main character in the story you have just read? On the lines below, list ten adjectives you could use to describe the character.

1. ______________________ **6.** ______________________

2. ______________________ **7.** ______________________

3. ______________________ **8.** ______________________

4. ______________________ **9.** ______________________

5. ______________________ **10.** ______________________

II. Which of these adjectives do you know to be appropriate because of something the character said? Write the adjective here: ______________________

Write the words the character said that showed you this was one of his or her traits here: ______________________

____

____

III. Which of the adjectives listed above do you know to be appropriate because of something the character did? Write the adjective here: ______________________

Write words from the story to show that you are correct here: ______________________

____

____

____

IV. Choose a third descriptive adjective that you know to be accurate as a result of what a second character said about the first character. Write the adjective here: ______________________

Write the words spoken by the second character here: ______________________

____

____

I Can Top That

Almost anything goes in this tall tale contest as long as the actions and reactions of the main character remain consistent.

Materials Needed

a description of a character, a setting, and an event

Instructions

Before Class

Prepare the description of a character, a setting, and an event.

During Class

1. Have students sit in a circle.
2. Tell students that
   - they are going to tell tall tales based on a given character and situation.
   - each time one student finishes, the next student must exclaim, "I can top that!" and continue with a bigger and better account of what happened.
   - the addition must not change the character's basic personality or include anything supernatural or totally impossible—only bigger and better.
3. Start the activity by reading this description:

The Valleyfield National Bank had been robbed more than a hundred years before, and the loot, a bag full of gold coins, had never been recovered. Brian had always laughed at the idea that the money might be hidden in Caravan Cave. Everyone knew that the mouth of the cave was blocked by huge boulders and the path which led to it was treacherous. Besides, Brian had always been quite sure those long-ago burglars had moved the money to a remote spot.

Such thoughts were far from Brian's mind as he carefully prepared for his hike. Collecting Indian arrowheads was a favorite hobby of his, and that morning was perfect for it. The boy quickly went through a mental checklist of the items he would need: canteen of water, shovel, empty bag, compass, and lunch—most of all, lunch. Before leaving the house, he wrote a note to his mother explaining where he was going and what he planned to do so that she would not be alarmed if she returned home before he did.

Brian's eyes surveyed the ground as he left the main path. He was not more than seventy-five feet from it when he felt the ground beneath his feet begin to give way. He landed on the floor of what he guessed must be Caravan Cave. And there, on the floor in front of him, was a gold coin . . .

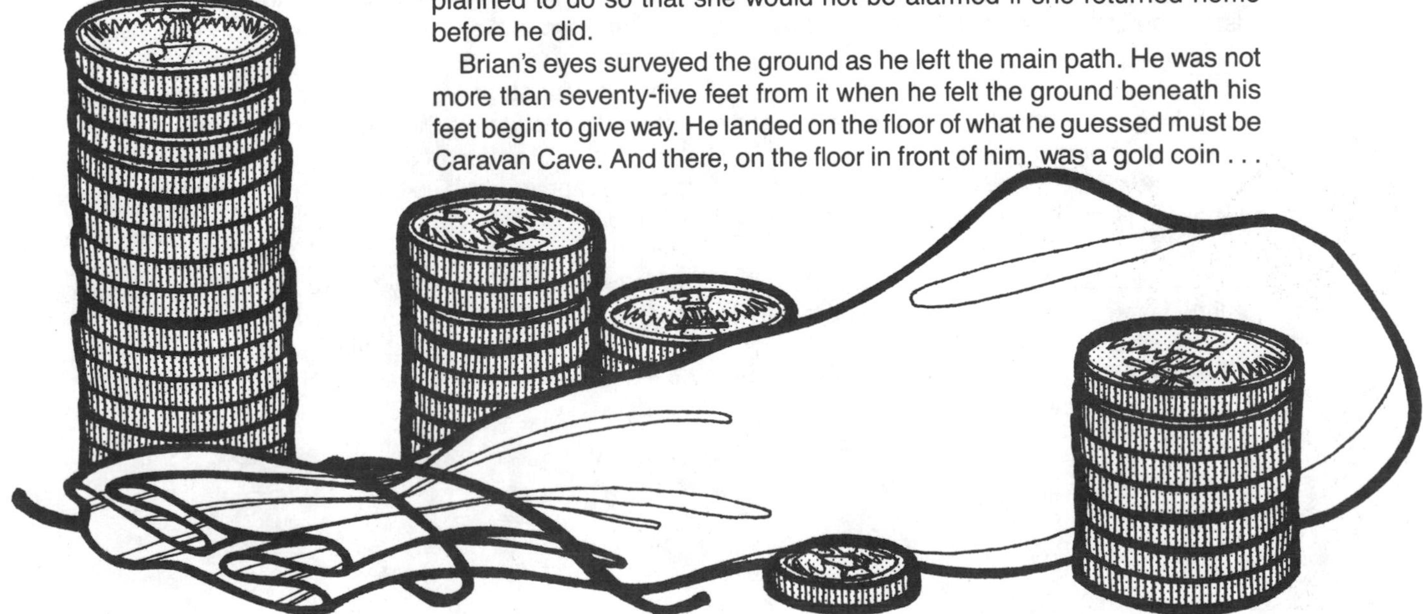

Name ____________________

Cases in Conflict

A **conflict** is a struggle. Every story includes at least one of the four main types of conflicts.

1. **Man vs. Man** involves a direct struggle between two of the characters in a story. Examples include a man and wife who disagree about how their money should be spent; two little boys engaged in a fistfight; a boss who is firing an employee.
2. **Man vs. Nature** involves a struggle between a character and elements of nature that are beyond his control. Examples are a family stranded by a snowstorm; a woman who is unable to function because of illness; a man stalked by a wild animal in the forest.
3. **Man vs. Society** involves the struggle between a character and the rules or laws that govern the society in which he lives. Examples are a woman who runs a red light; a child who plays hooky; a burglar who breaks into a house.
4. **Man vs. Himself** involves the struggle between the character and his conscience. Examples are a woman who is tempted to steal money from her employer; a child who cannot decide whether or not to lie to his mother about his reason for arriving home late; a man who would like to quit his job.

Identify the type of conflict in each of the following paragraphs.

1. ____________________ After only two days of summer vacation, Joshua and Sam were already bored, so they decided to kill some time by walking down to Judson's Variety, Smithfield's five-and-ten-cent store. Because Sam had no money with him, he could only eye the rack that held the Chocolate Craters, his favorite candy bar. Maybe no one would notice if he slipped one into his pocket.

2. ____________________ The big day had finally arrived, and Ron was on his way to see Mr. Desmond for an interview. This was the chance of a lifetime; he might actually be appointed vice-president of Desmond Diamonds, International. After donning his rain coat and kissing his wife good-bye, he raced through the rain to his car. As he neared the Chester Corners Bridge, he could see that traffic was at a standstill. The bridge was out! What would Mr. Desmond think when Ron didn't show up for the interview?

3. ____________________ The house was perfect, totally hidden from prying eyes. After checking to be sure that the garage was empty, Rusty stole around to the back of the house, where he had no trouble jimmying the sliding glass door. He found nothing of value on the living room shelves; but at the back of the closet in the master bedroom, he discovered the prized coin collection. This single discovery might make it possible for him to retire from his life of crime.

4. ____________________ "This is silly," thought Sandy to himself as he started to walk a little faster down Fifth Street. "Who would possibly want to follow me?" But the harder he listened, the more positive he became that someone was approaching him from behind. Suddenly, a strong arm spun him around. Sandy stared in disbelief but had no time for a response before the masked stranger slugged him and knocked him down.

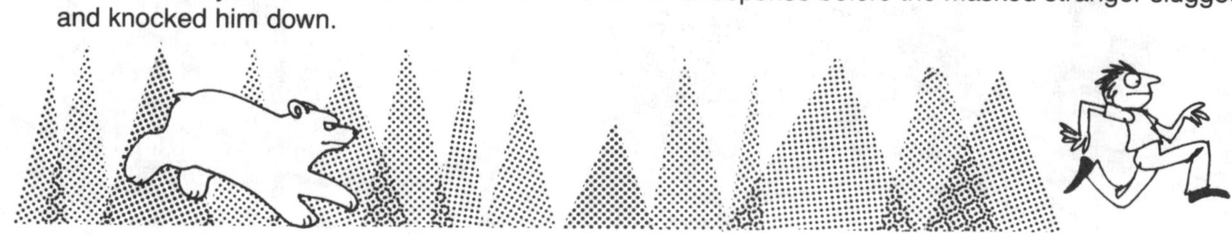

Name ____________________

Conflict Capers

This setting and cast of characters have no place to go. It is up to you to get them moving. For each type of conflict listed, create a different plot synopsis. Explain the conflict and how it will be resolved. The first one has been done for you.

Setting: Muston, Oklahoma, in 1949
Characters: Rona Burke, age seven
Delia Burke, her mother
Elmer Burke, her father, a farmer
Colin Parker, a stranger

1. **Man vs. Society:** When the Burkes had first taken in Colin Parker on that rainy night in May, they had no idea he was a fugitive from the law. As their affection and respect for the youth grew, they were torn by the gravity of the choice they must make: Should they, as law-abiding citizens, report the boy, or should they, as friends whose respect and affection Colin had won, protect him? Because of their concern for Rona's values, they finally decided to tell Colin that they must report him but that they were willing to post bail and to stand by him during the ordeal that lay ahead.
2. **Man vs. Himself:** ____________________
3. **Man vs. Man:** ____________________
4. **Man vs. Nature:** ____________________

Name ____________________

Focus on Flashback

> A **flashback** is an interruption in a story to permit the author to relate an event from the past.

Detective Tyler Mills felt the gun press harshly against the side of his head. "Oh, oh," he thought, "TROUBLE!" Minutes later he found himself bound, gagged, and alone in a dark corner of the warehouse.

After a few minutes of useless struggling, Mills admitted to himself that it was hopeless; he was trapped until someone chose to free him. With a sigh, he settled himself as comfortably as possible and let his mind wander back to the events that had led to his current predicament.

He had received the first phone call about three days earlier. A husky voice offered key information on a drug ring Mills had been investigating for months. The caller promised to give him names, dates of planned shipments—the works—but only if the price was right. The call ended abruptly, before it could be traced by police personnel. Late that night, this time at his home, Mills had received another phone call. The caller demanded $500, gave a post office box number, and once again hung up abruptly. Mills had debated for a few minutes, and then decided that the opportunity was too important to pass up. He had posted the money, at the same time staking out the post office in the hope of apprehending the informer. That attempt failed, and he heard nothing for the next twenty-four hours. Then, this morning, he had received the third call. This time the caller agreed to meet with Mills, giving him the address of the warehouse where he now lay. It was obvious that the whole thing had been a trap, and Mills cursed his own stupidity.

Number the events below in the order in which they actually occurred—in chronological order. Then letter the same events in the order in which they are described in this narrative.

Chronological Order	Narrative Order	
___	___	Mills received the second phone call.
___	___	Mills decided the calls had been a trap.
___	___	Mills began investigating a drug ring.
___	___	Mills found himself tied and gagged.
___	___	Mills received the first phone call.
___	___	Mills staked out the post office.
___	___	Mills went to the abandoned warehouse.
___	___	Mills posted the $500 to the informer.
___	___	Mills realized he could not free himself.
___	___	Mills decided to "take a chance" on the informer.

II. Underline the words in the narrative that introduced the flashback.

Name ______________________

What's the Purpose?

The **author's purpose** is the author's intent in writing a piece of prose or poetry.

Read the excerpts below. Decide what purpose the author had in mind for each one. Was it to describe, to entertain, to inform, or to persuade? Write the purpose for each excerpt on the line below it.

There is a new business in town at 131 Main Street. The Dead-On Detective Agency will open its doors for the first time today. Owned and operated by Timothy Johns, a former police officer, the agency will offer a variety of private investigatory services. Mr. Johns assures us that any investigations he undertakes will be completed quickly and in complete confidence. Prospective clients may call 786-0329 to arrange an appointment. We wish Mr. Johns luck in his new business, and welcome him to Boise City.

I. ______________________

DEAD-ON DETECTIVE AGENCY
QUICK - PRIVATE - INEXPENSIVE
No problem too small or too big!
CALL 786-0329 TODAY!

II. ______________________

The outer door of the Dead-On Detective Agency opened. A young woman looked timidly about, then stepped inside. Timothy Johns looked up from the desk where he was working and smiled. The young woman moved hesitantly toward him, then perched herself primly on the edge of a chair in front of his desk. "Mr. Johns," she began, "I . . . I'm in trouble."

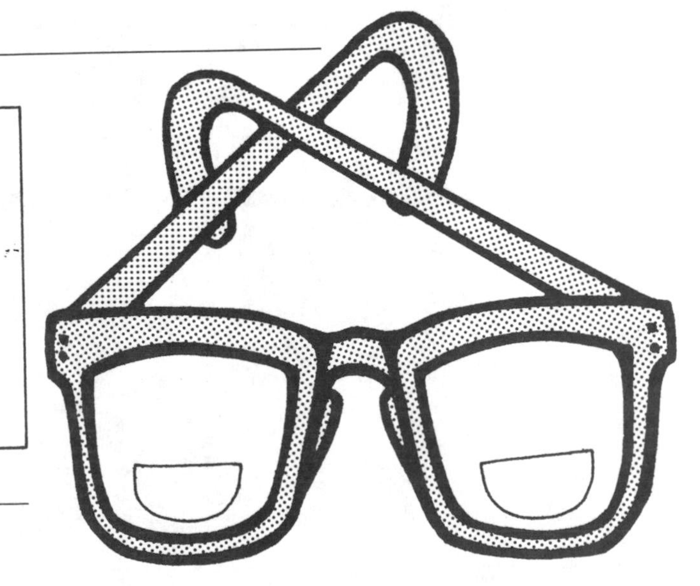

III. ______________________

Name ____________________

From the Outside Looking In

Point of view is the voice the author uses to tell the story. It may be **first person**, in which the author is a character in the story and tells it from his or her point of view.

Example: I've never been as frightened as I was last Friday night. I was walking home from work when I heard footsteps behind me.

It may be **third person objective**, in which the author is not a character in the story and is only able to report actions. This point of view is most often used in newspaper stories.

Example: Someone was following Mary on her way home from work Friday night.

It may be **third person omniscient**, in which the author is not a character in the story but is able to look into the characters' minds and report what they are thinking.

Example: As Mary hurried home from work Friday night, she felt panicked by the sound of footsteps behind her.

Ben Hawkins has a clear view of the situation as he relates the following paragraphs in the first person:

The Huntington case had me stumped for months, so I was thoroughly delighted when a weapon was discovered and brought to me by a group of Girl Scouts who had been camping for the weekend in the woods behind the Huntingtons' house. This could break the case wide open and give me a big break in my career as well! I'd had to wait a long time for an office of my own with the words "Ben Hawkins, Chief Detective" stenciled in gold letters on the door.

On a separate sheet of paper, rewrite this paragraph in third person objective and then in third person omniscient.

Name ______________________

The Tone at the Time Is . . .

Tone is the style or manner of expression in speaking or writing. It reflects the author's attitude toward the material.

Justice Thwarted

We have learned today that Bill Able, a youth involved in an armed robbery and assault on an innocent citizen only three months ago, is to be freed at the end of this month. The reason? Able will turn eighteen at that time and by law must be released and returned to society. This is a serious issue and should be of concern to all of us.

This "child," by his own admission, robbed the Elm Tree General Store at gunpoint and severely beat Gus Erickson, the proprietor. There is no question, moreover, that Able was fully cognizant of right and wrong at the time he took the actions he did. His motive for the robbery was, again by his own admission, greed; for the assault, malice. Able spoke openly of his dislike for Erickson, a man who reprimanded Able on several occasions for his behavior outside Erickson's store.

Yet this "child," because of concern by juvenile authorities and because of a seriously flawed judicial system, will go free. He will be free to terrorize, to assault—in short, to commit precisely the same kinds of crimes for which he served only three short months in jail.

It is time to plug the loophole in our law that allows a youth like this to escape the consequences of his actions, a flaw that permits anyone under the age of eighteen to hurt persons and destroy property without fear of long-term retribution. It's time we spoke up!

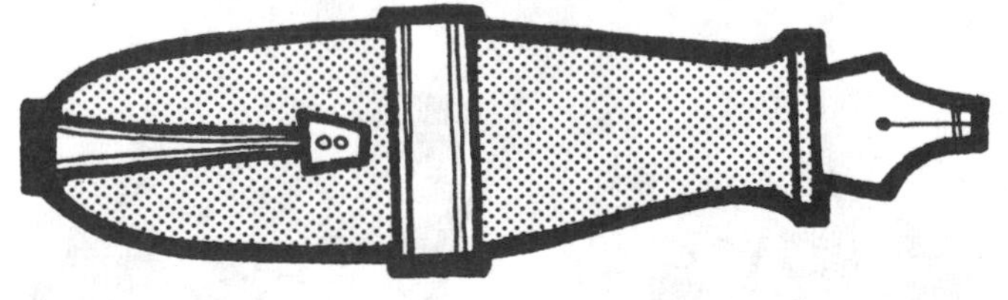

Happy Birthday to One But Not to All

We were pleased to learn today that Bill Able, a youth involved in an armed robbery and assault on an innocent citizen three long months ago, is to be freed at the end of this month in time for his eighteenth birthday. How appropriate! After all, no child should miss his birthday.

1. What audience does the author address in this editorial? ______________________
2. What attitude does he or she express toward Able? ______________________
3. What attitude does he or she convey toward juvenile law? ______________________
4. Is the tone of this editorial admiring, amused, angry, resentful, or triumphant? ______________________

Rewrite the editorial in the right-hand column to express the same attitudes but in a sarcastic tone. This editorial has been begun for you.

Name ______________________________

Setting Sampler

Setting is the time and place in which an event occurs.

Read the passages below and answer the questions that follow.

I. His black leather jacket snugged tight around him, his hair slicked back, he arrogantly mounted his cycle and headed down Main Street. Along the way he could see clusters of teens, their faces reflected in the illuminated shop windows. Friends cruised by in cars, honking or waving as they passed. Brad's face was set in a determined expression as he continued on his way toward the Sand Pit. He knew Jim would be waiting there. This was it—the showdown!

1. *When does the scene take place? At approximately what time of day? Circle the words that tell you this.*
2. *Where does the scene take place? Underline the words that tell you this.*
3. *Where will the next scene take place? How important do you think this setting will be to the story? Why?*

II. The sound of the riverboat whistle brought the town to life. A bell pealed, and scores of beribboned girls and knicker-clad boys cascaded from the schoolhouse door and headed for the river. On the docks, men hurried to and fro, hauling huge bundles of cotton and large wooden crates. The boat loomed larger now, its decks filled with waving men and women. The captain stood somberly in the pilothouse, his attention focused on the task at hand.

1. *During what period in American history does the story take place? Circle the words that tell you this.*
2. *In what part of the country does the story take place? Underline the words that tell you this.*

III. The crowd numbered more than 50,000, and nervous officials paced outside the fence. Inside, dogs and children romped, and long-haired students raced about playing Frisbee, waiting for the concert to begin. Some sat talking in small groups. Late risers piled sleeping bags and belongings together. All mingled with the chaotic noise and confusion. The bright colors worn by the participants created a mosaic effect. Peace signs were scrawled everywhere. The atmosphere was alive and expectant.

1. *When do you think the story takes place?*
2. *Do you think the specific location will be important to this story? Why or why not?*

Name ____________________

Verbal Imagery

> **Verbal imagery** is vivid figurative language used to create a clear word picture.

It is vitally important that the reader be able to picture the setting of a suspenseful story. Here is a chance to learn how good you are at verbal imagery—creating a clear word picture.

The drawing at the top of this page shows a time and place that are typical for many spooky stories. On the lines below, write a description of this setting. Make your words create a picture so that a reader who has not seen the place will be able to visualize it as clearly as you can. A thesaurus may be helpful.

____

____

____

____

____

____

____

____

____

Cut out your description. Have a friend read it and draw a picture of the scene it brings to mind. To measure your descriptive writing skills, compare your friend's picture with the picture you described. Did you leave out any important details?

Paper Bag Create-a-Story

Four clues in a paper bag prompt imaginative thinking in this writing activity. Aided by these clues and a Create-a-Story Worksheet, students work in groups to create spell-binding mystery stories.

Materials Needed

one paper bag for each group of four students
a group of four unrelated objects to place in each bag
a copy of the Create-a-Story Worksheet on page 55 for each student

Instructions

Before Class

1. Secure enough paper bags so that you have one bag for each group of four students.
2. Put four unrelated objects in each paper bag. For example, you might put a torn scrap of paper money, a bobbypin, a small length of rope, and a burned match in one bag.
3. Duplicate enough copies of the Create-a-Story Worksheet so that each member of the class can have one.

During Class

1. Divide the class into groups of four.
2. Give each group one bag and four worksheets.
3. Go over the worksheet instructions with the class as a whole.
4. Allow the members of each group to work together to create a mystery story in which all four objects are vital to the solution.

Follow-up

Groups may read their stories aloud, bind them in folders for inclusion in the classroom or school library, or turn them into radio plays complete with sound effects.

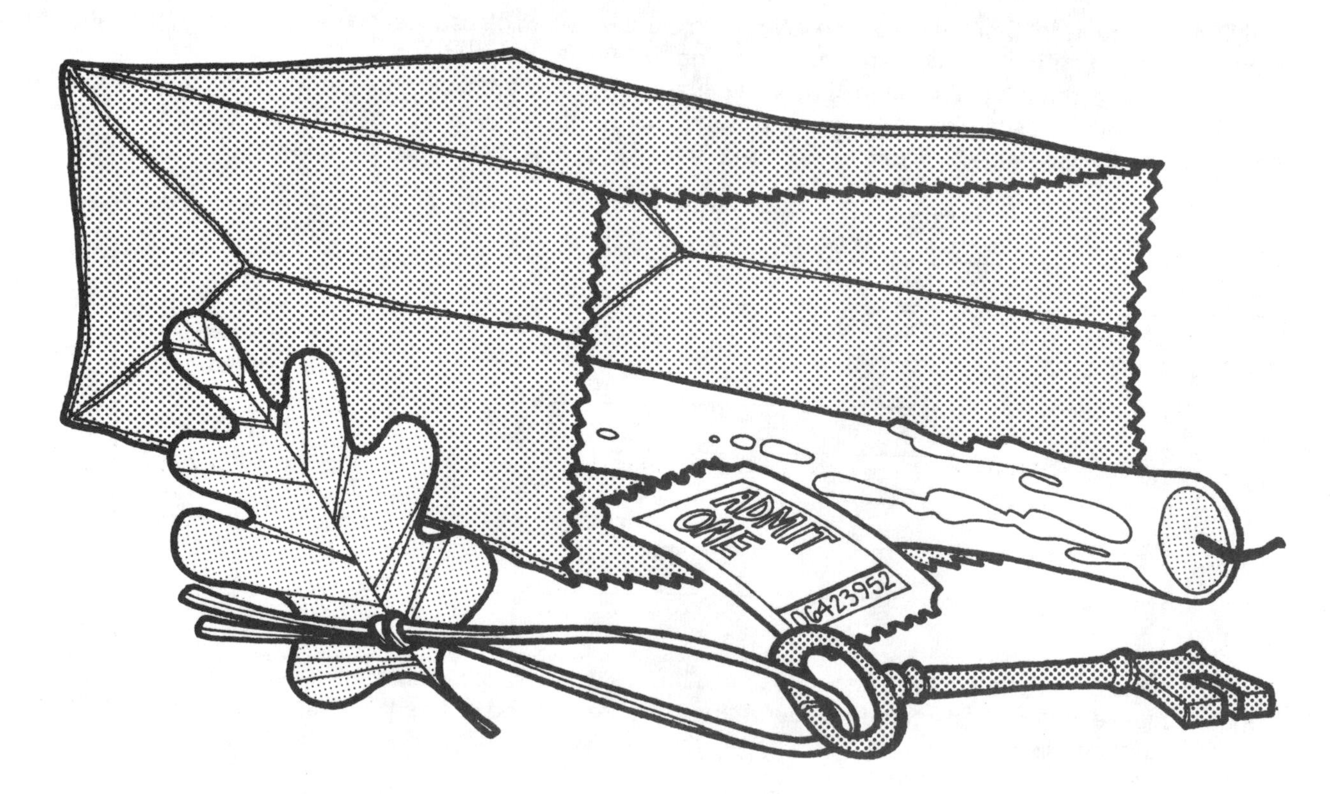

Name ______________________

Create-a-Story Worksheet

Attention,future mystery writers! Have you ever wished to follow in the footsteps of Ellery Queen or Agatha Christie, writing exciting, well-constructed mysteries for eager readers to enjoy? Here's your chance. The paper bag in front of you contains four clues that are vital to the solution of a mystery you are going to create. Follow these simple, step-by-step instructions, and you'll produce a story that is almost certain to fascinate mystery lovers.

I. Select a setting from the list below and underline it, or create your own setting and name or describe it.

the desert	the slopes of Mount Everest
the basement of a rundown apartment house	the turret of a abandoned castle
an island in the Pacific Ocean	a schoolroom

other ______________________

II. Open your bag and list your four clues.

	Clues	**Possible Meanings**
1.	____________	____________
2.	____________	____________
3.	____________	____________
4.	____________	____________

III. What could each clue mean in the setting you have selected? Write one possible meaning for each clue.

IV. In what kind of crime might all four clues be involved? ______________________

____

V. What was the motive for this crime? Choose a motive from the list below and underline it, or think up your own motive and name or describe it.

fame	love	power
greed	jealousy	revenge

other ______________________

VI. You will need a cast of characters—a villain, a victim, and a hero (the detective who solves the crime). To cast your story, complete these bags. Use another sheet of paper if you need more space.

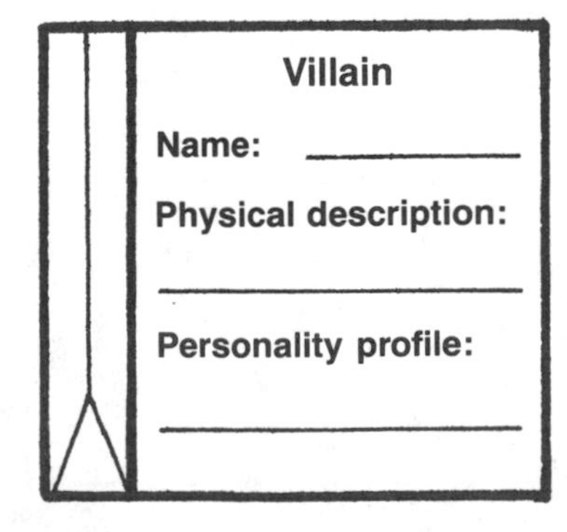

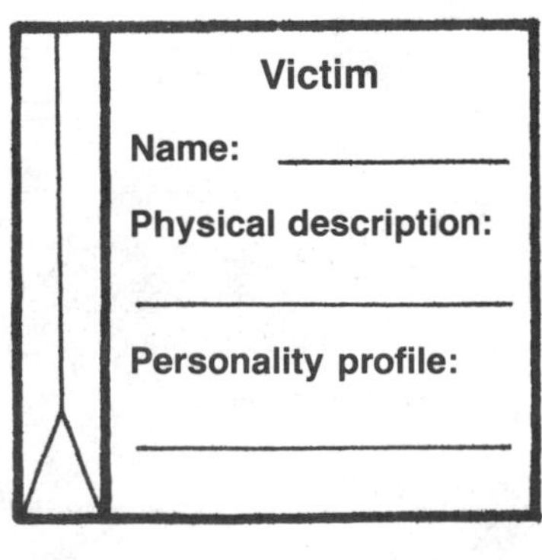

Detective

Name: ____________

Physical description:

____

Personality profile:

____

VII. With one member of your group acting as scribe or secretary, involve the characters you have described and the clues you were given in a mystery that takes place in the setting you have selected to create a spell-binding story.

Name ______________________

Mood Messages

Mood is the feeling an author wishes to create for the reader. Mood may be created by means of setting, situation, or description separately, or by any combination of these elements.

I. Setting: It was a cold, dreary night. Storm clouds hung low in the sky, the wind moaned, and the moon flitted in and out, casting shifting shadows. The house stood deserted. Its sagging shutters beat time to the puffs of wind. Moss dripped from its clapboards like the webs of a hundred ancient spiders. The broken steps pointed the way to a long-disused door.

1. *How does the author wish you to feel?*

____

____

2. *Underline the words that create this effect.*

3. *What would happen if you substituted more cheerful language?*

____

____

4. *Try it and see. On a separate sheet of paper, rewrite the paragraph to change the mood.*

II. Situation: Sara hurried along, her brisk footsteps resounding on the pavement. She moved quickly, past deserted storefronts and narrow alleyways. Her breath came in short gasps, and her heart pounded loudly. Then she heard it—a short "ping"—a sound instantly gone and followed only by silence. She clutched the precious package more tightly to her body and began to run.

1. *What few details about the setting does the author provide?*

____

____

____

____

2. *What is the situation in which Sara finds herself?*

____

____

____

____

3. *What mood is the author of this passage trying to create?*

____

____

____

____

Name ______________________________

Mood Messages
(continued)

III. Description: He had known all along that it would be a disaster. For an unknown sixteen-year-old to defeat cyclists who were so much more experienced simply was not possible.

With these thoughts in mind, John bent lower over his handlebars, his calf muscles throbbing as his legs moved rhythmically up and down. The road stretched unendingly before him, and in the far distance he could just make out the smug forms of the race leaders.

1. *In this passage the author provides a verbal description of the main character's mood. Underline those sentences that specifically state how John was feeling.*

2. *What description of the setting does the author provide?*

____

____

____

3. *Circle any words in the author's description of the setting that are "colored" by John's frame of mind.*

Name ____________________

Mood Magic

When movie producers adapt a story for the screen, they use words, music, and photography to create the mood. For example, witty conversation and hard rock music would be totally inappropriate for most funeral scenes; sober words and somber music would probably be used instead.

You, too, can use words, music, and photography or art to produce a particular mood. Simply follow these steps.

1. Working alone or with a partner, decide what mood you would like to evoke. Identify or describe it on the lines below.

Mood: ____________________

2. Select a poem, a musical composition, and a drawing or photograph that can work together to produce the feeling you have in mind. Identify them by title or brief description on the lines below.

Poem: ____________________

Music: ____________________

Drawing or Photograph: ____________________

3. Display the illustration and read the poem to the class while the music you have selected is played quietly in the background.

4. Ask your classmates to identify the mood you have created. What mood did *they* feel?

____

Was it the same mood *you* were trying to create?

____

Why or why not? ____________________

If you were to do the same activity again, what would you do differently to make your mood creation more effective?

____

Name ______________________________

Figuratively Speaking

Figurative language is any language that is used creatively and imaginatively to evoke vivid images and to give fresh insights.

With a scream as of pain, the siren echoed in the night. The staccato of a machine gun was heard spitting bullets at figures scurrying away, crablike, into the sheltering darkness. With bodies hunched in fear, they scuttled and dodged, trying to avoid the threatening tentacles of barbed wire that tore at their clothing. Lights flashed, writing a crazed calligraphy across the ink-black sky. Then, in an instant, it was over. The tide of noise and motion subsided until only silence and darkness remained. The border was quiet once again.

1. *List briefly the events described in this paragraph.*

a. ______________________________

b. ______________________________

c. ______________________________

d. ______________________________

e. ______________________________

f. ______________________________

2. *Explain the meaning of each of the following groups of words as it is used in the paragraph.*

a. *with a scream as of pain*

____

____

b. *the staccato of a machine gun*

____

____

____

c. *spitting bullets*

____

d. *scurrying away, crablike, into the sheltering darkness*

____

____

____

____

e. *as they scuttled and dodged*

____

____

____

f. *threatening tentacles of barbed wire tore at their clothing*

____

____

g. *writing a crazed calligraphy across the ink-black sky*

____

____

____

h. *the tide of noise and motion subsided*

____

____

3. *On a separate sheet of paper, rewrite the paragraph, substituting literal language for the figurative language used by the author. When you do so, what happens to the paragraph?*

____

4. *Which paragraph is more vivid, yours or the author's?*

____

Why? ______________________________

____

____

Name ______________________________

Symbol Search

A **symbol** is an object, person, place, or event that can be used to stand for, represent, or suggest something else because of traditional association, emotional content, or accidental resemblance. For example, an apple may be used to suggest school because of traditional association. For the same reason, a four-leaf clover symbolizes good luck.

I. You have just opened your own detective agency. In the space on the right, create a business card for yourself complete with a slogan and a symbol, or logo.

II. You have been asked by the Crime Capers Publishing Company to create symbols for the story categories in their mystery and suspense line. The categories are detective, ghost, horror, locked room, murder, psychological thriller, and spy. In the boxes on the right and below, design a symbol for each category.

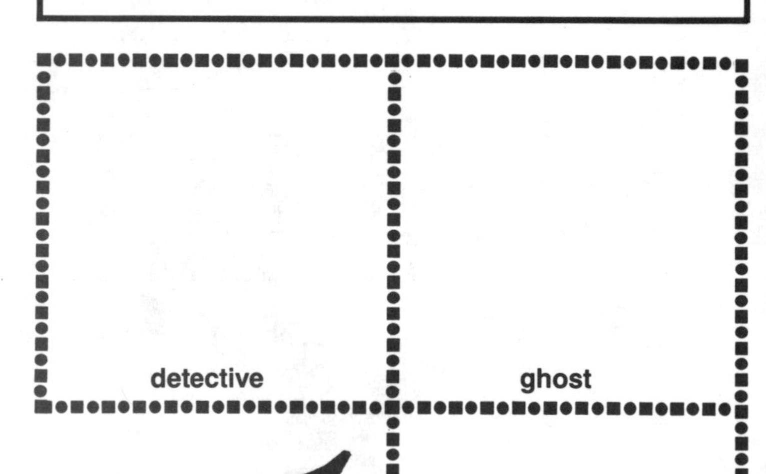

horror

locked room	murder	psychological thriller	spy

Name ________________________________

The Context Connection

Context clues are familiar words that help the reader determine the meanings of other, unfamiliar words. There are four important kinds of context clues. In the examples of each kind given below, the word is underlined and the context clue is set in **boldface** type.

1. **Restatement**—a clue provided by including a synonym or definition so that the reader is actually given the meaning of the word.
   Example: They hung the noose, **a loop with a slipknot**, from the rafter.
2. **Example**—a clue provided by including examples.
   Example: The forensic equipment included **examining tables, surgical tools,** and a **fingerprinting kit.**
3. **Comparison**—a clue provided by comparing two seemingly unrelated things so that the meaning of one of them will be clarified.
   Example: The suspect's guilt was as blatant as **a professional basketball player in the midst of a group of midgets.**
4. **Contrast**—a clue provided by including a contrast that underscores what the word does *not* mean.
   Example: The supposed **poison was harmless,** but the antidote **proved venomous.**

Read the sentences below. On the line beside each one, indicate by number the kind of context clue that is given and write what you think the underlined word means.

1. The suspect talked incessantly, while the detective remained silent. — 1. ________________________
2. He thought of various means of retribution for the wrong done to him—an anonymous letter, public embarrassment, or even physical violence. — 2. ________________________
3. His field was espionage, or more precisely, surveillance. — 3. ________________________
4. The painstaking detective was the antithesis of his careless superior. — 4. ________________________
5. The townsfolk could not sanction killing, so they ordered the marshal to bring the accused man in alive. — 5. ________________________
6. It was impossible for the settled, well-to-do gentleman to understand the life the vagrant led. — 6. ________________________

When you have finished, check your answers against the meanings given in a dictionary for the underlined words. Give yourself one point for each correct answer. Then rate yourself as follows:

5 or 6 points	=	a verbal live wire
3 or 4 points	=	not quite fully charged
below 3 points	=	some dead cells in the verbal battery

What is your score? ____________________ How do you rate? ____________________

Multiple Meanings Mystique

Using drawings, photographs, magazine clippings, and written descriptions, students create collages for a multiple meanings bulletin board.

Materials Needed

old magazines that students can cut up
white unlined paper
colored construction paper
scissors, pencils, pens, crayons
glue
word cards
bag, hat, or can to hold cards

Instructions

Before Class Cut apart the word cards at the bottom of this page and place them in a bag, hat, or can.

During Class

1. Explain multiple meanings to students. The words **space** and **pin** may be used as examples.
2. Have each student select a word.
3. Ask each student to create a collage, using the materials you have provided, that represents the multiple meanings of the word he or she has selected.

Follow-up Create a multiple meanings bulletin board on which you display the students' collages.

set	duck	frame	fine
strike	air	mine	story
flight	round	press	sound
race	match	cool	pen
free	fence	fly	miss

Name ________________________________

Pick a Prefix

A **prefix** is a word part that is added to the front of a base or root word to change its meaning.

Help your vocabulary branch out. On the leaves at the ends of each prefix limb, write words that have been created by combining that prefix with base or root words.

Name ______________________________

Eye Spy Suffixes

> A **suffix** is a word part that is added to the end of a base or root word to change its meaning. Usually the part of speech is changed as well. Sometimes the spelling of the base or root word must be changed when the suffix is added.

Keep your eye on the suffix and you'll end up with an eyeful of good words. Match the base words in the box with an appropriate suffix or two. Write each new word you create in this way in the appropriate suffix eye.

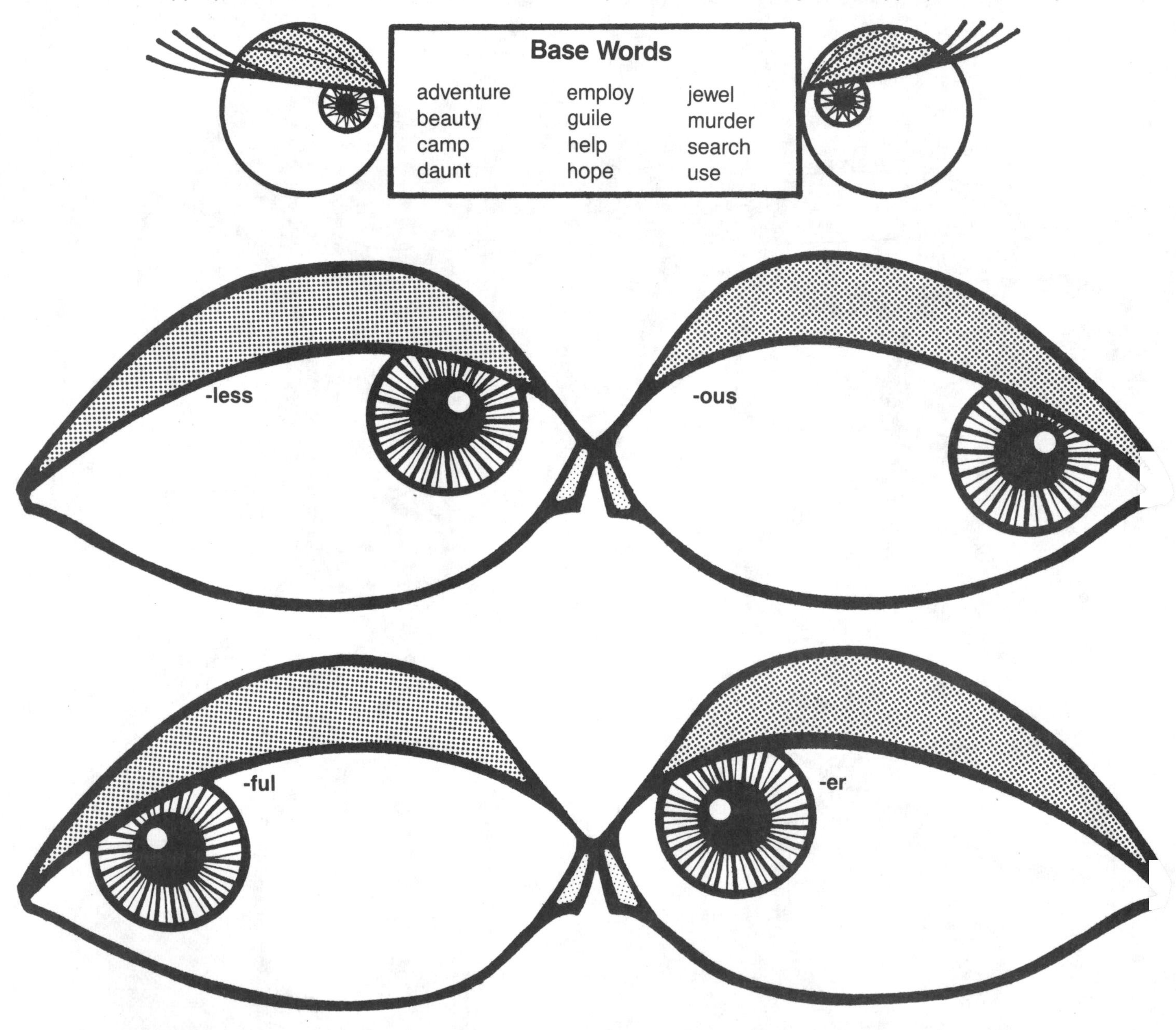

Take a look at the words you have created. Figure out the meaning of each suffix. Write that meaning in each eye next to the suffix. Then look up each suffix in a dictionary to be sure that you are right.

Name ______________________

Would You If You Could?

Are you mystified by the questions below? Use your dictionary to look up the meanings of any words you do not know. Answer each question by writing **yes** or **no** on the line beside it.

1. Would you expect a burglar to be **indicted**? ______
2. Would you expect **remuneration** for your detective work? ______
3. Would you **seethe** if you had just won an important case? ______
4. Would you present your **dossier** to a suspect? ______
5. Would you **berate** a policeman for helping you? ______
6. Would you be **doleful** if you received a reward? ______
7. Would you seek **notoriety** if you were guilty of a crime? ______
8. Would you lubricate your car with **liniment**? ______
9. Would you look **emaciated** if you had been on a prolonged hunger strike? ______
10. Would you **acquiesce** if you wanted to make things easier for the prosecution? ______

On the lines below, write five questions for a friend to answer.

1. ______________________
2. ______________________
3. ______________________
4. ______________________
5. ______________________

Detectionary

The dictionary becomes a very popular tool when groups of students try this game. Through it they will learn the parts of a dictionary entry.

Materials Needed

a dictionary for each group of students
index cards
a pencil for each student

Instructions

Before Class

Introduce and explain the parts of a dictionary entry: alternate spellings (if there are any), syllabication, pronounciation, part of speech, derivation, and meanings.

During Class

1. Divide the class into groups of five or six.
2. Appoint one member of each group to be the first detective.
3. Each detective uses the dictionary to find a word that he thinks will be unfamiliar to the other members of his group. He announces the word to the group.
4. Each member of the group makes up a plausible dictionary entry for the word and writes it on an index card.
5. At the same time, the detective writes out the true dictionary entry for the word on another index card.
6. The detective collects all of the entries for the word.
7. The detective reads the imaginary and real dictionary entries.
8. The members of the group vote for the entry that they believe is the real one.
9. The detective reveals the real meaning of the word.
10. The detective passes the dictionary to the team member on his right, who becomes the next detective.
11. The game continues until each member of the group has had a chance to be the detective.

MOZO SAYYID OXTER
VUG WOADWAX BHUT DEX
QUINCUNX ZOIC FILIBEC
FOURCHÉE CLEEK THYMY AA
JO XYLYL OKA
EPIGYNY
APHYLLY RINK

Name ______________________________

Target Practice

Are you on target in your use of descriptive words? Place each word targeted below in a sentence. Award yourself five points for each correct hit.

1. After a ________________ glance at the brawny gentleman approaching him with his fists raised, the fainthearted fellow ran away.
2. The poison was very ________________; after ingesting it, he was dead within seconds.
3. The moment he entered the carefully devised trap, he knew he was ________________.
4. The ________________ gentleman became too greedy and was convicted of embezzlement.
5. The investigator decided that because time was of the essence, it would be ________________ to call rather than visit.
6. The ________________ look in Holmes's eye told Watson he was wrong—again.
7. The ________________ Sherlock Holmes enjoyed the recognition he received wherever he went.
8. The ________________ crowd surged toward the prison door, completely out of control.
9. The pain from his wound was ________________; for a few moments, he lost consciousness.
10. The ________________ boy delighted in tormenting timid children.
11. A celebration was held to mark the ________________ occasion.
12. With a ________________ grin, he began to repeat a completely unfounded rumor.
13. The ________________ look on his father's face convinced the boy he should remain silent.
14. The detective cast a ________________ glance at the suspect, who winced.
15. Even though he was ________________, he refused to turn to a life of crime.
16. The villain's face was so ________________, no one wished to look at it.
17. The ________________ prisoner had not been fed anything but bread and water for months.
18. Because he knew arrest was ________________, he fled the country.
19. He was ________________ about entering the building unarmed.
20. The timid officer found the ________________ old gentleman very difficult to question.

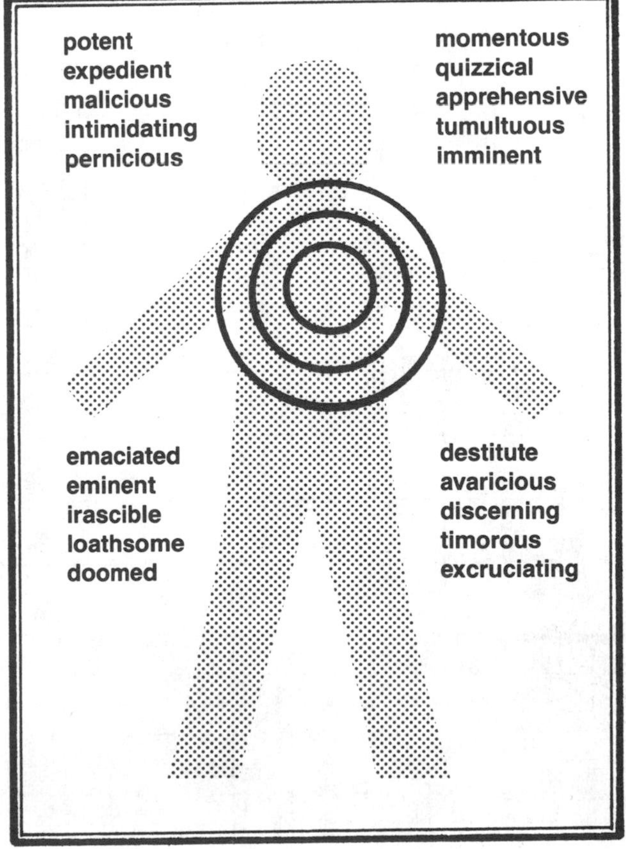

Name ____________________

Doublecross

Every good investigator must be on the lookout for a doublecross. To get the jump on your opponent, follow these simple instructions.

1. Write some of the words from the word list in the squares below to make a crossword puzzle.
2. Add other short words as needed so that the puzzle words intersect and letters are shared between them.
3. Shade or blacken the blank squares.
4. Beginning with the top row and moving horizontally from left to right, number every square in which a word begins.
5. On a separate sheet of paper, write a clue, synonym, or definition for each word.
6. Number each word clue to match the square in which that word begins.
7. Write the clues in numerical order on the lines at the top of the Doublecross Puzzle Page (page 69). List clues for words that go across under the **Across** heading and clues for words that go down under the **Down** heading.
8. Number the squares on the Doublecross Puzzle Page to correspond to the squares on your puzzle.
9. Give the completed puzzle page to your opponent and watch him or her wrestle with your Doublecross.

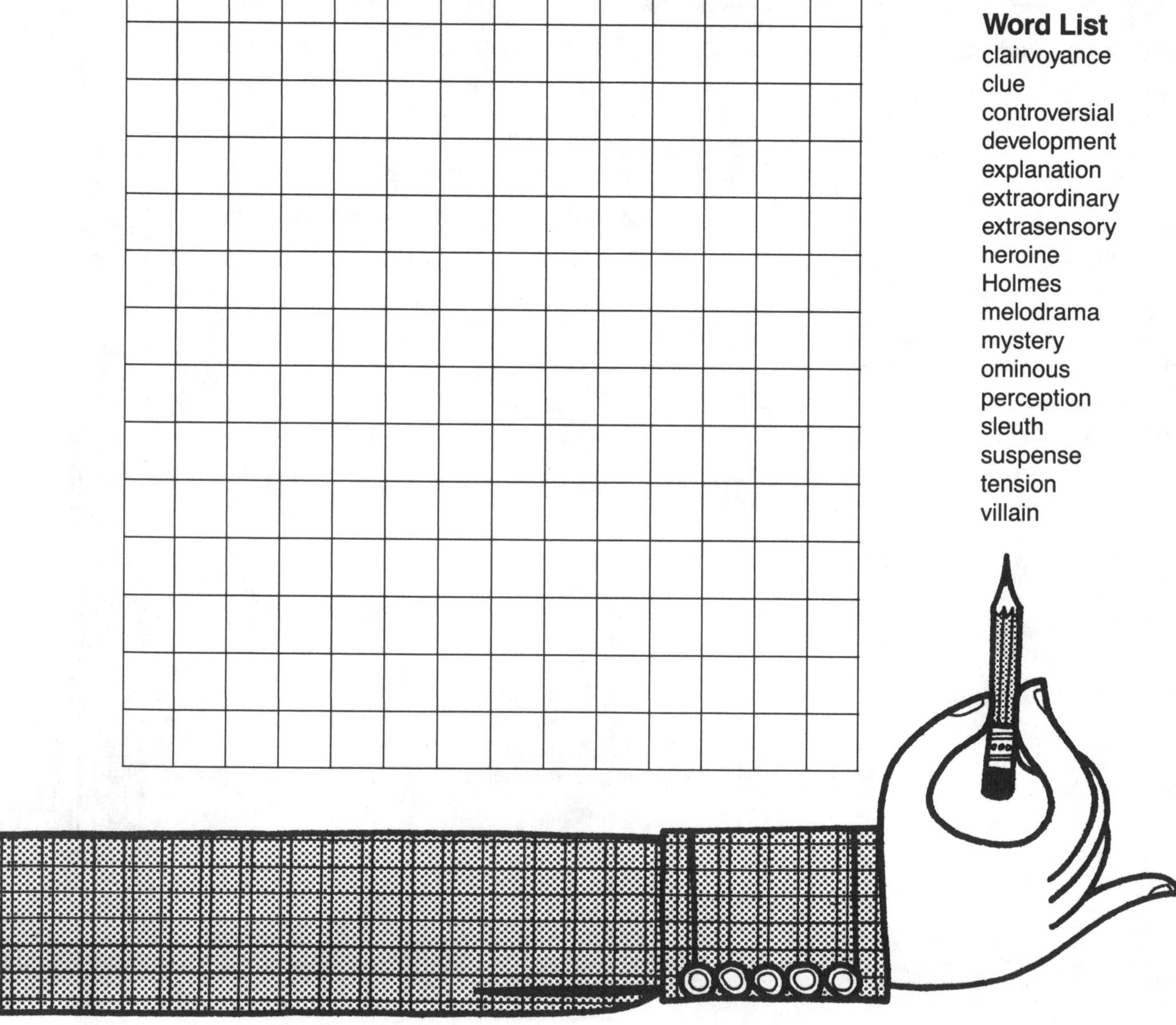

Word List
clairvoyance
clue
controversial
development
explanation
extraordinary
extrasensory
heroine
Holmes
melodrama
mystery
ominous
perception
sleuth
suspense
tension
villain

Name ______________________

Doublecross Puzzle Page

Across

____
____
____
____
____
____
____
____
____
____

Down

____
____
____
____
____
____
____
____
____
____

Name ________________________________

Try the Thesaurus

Tessy Russ, the famous writer of detective novels, is working on her next best seller. She knows that the reading public won't stand for dull, uninteresting work. Help Ms. Russ improve the sentence below. Use your thesaurus to find three more vivid substitutes for the underlined words.

	Good	Better	Best
"I			
stopped	____________	____________	____________
the			
burglar	____________	____________	____________
as he			
went	____________	____________	____________
toward the			
door,"	____________	____________	____________
said	____________	____________	____________
Lieutenant			
Purrington.			

Name ____________________

Get in the Synonym Spirit

> **Synonyms** are words that have the same or very similar meanings. For example, a synonym for *large* is *big*.

The spirit below contains thirteen pairs of synonyms. When you find them, list them on the lines provided at the bottom of the page. You may use the dictionary to help you in your search.

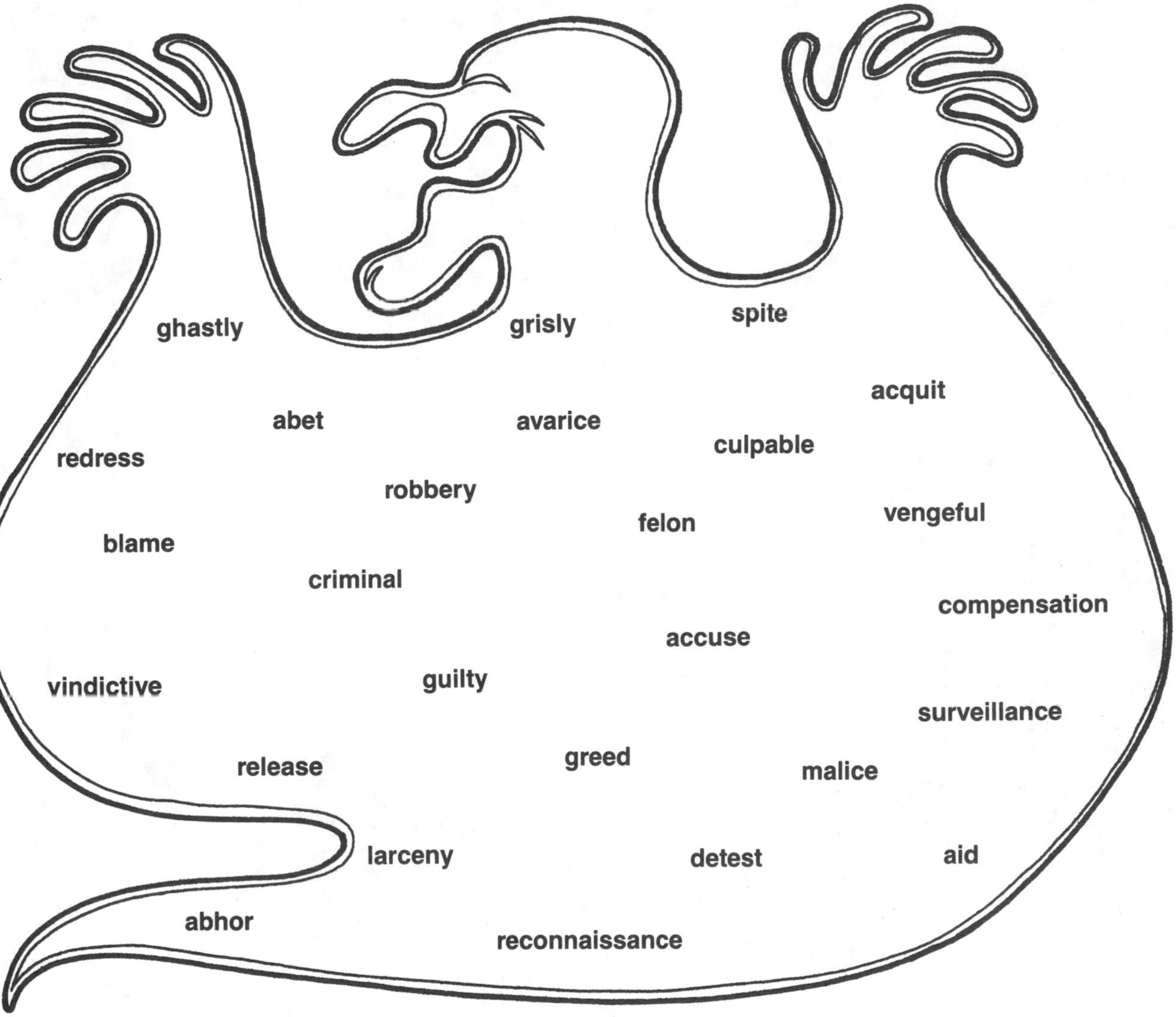

1. ______ ______
2. ______ ______
3. ______ ______
4. ______ ______
5. ______ ______
6. ______ ______
7. ______ ______
8. ______ ______
9. ______ ______
10. ______ ______
11. ______ ______
12. ______ ______
13. ______ ______

Name ______________________

Double Trouble

Can you detect a double? The box below is loaded with words from the Target Practice on page 67. Find the words and circle them. Then write each word next to its synonym, or double, at the bottom of the page.

Q	A	T	I	S	U	O	I	C	I	N	R	E	P	A	G
U	H	I	J	E	X	C	R	U	C	I	A	T	I	N	G
I	A	M	E	E	M	A	C	I	A	T	E	D	S	Y	E
Z	G	O	B	X	V	P	F	N	Q	R	D	T	U	Y	F
Z	C	R	D	P	E	T	W	T	E	N	E	V	A	R	C
I	A	O	G	E	C	I	A	I	M	D	S	O	L	W	I
C	F	U	I	D	F	O	E	M	O	I	T	K	M	N	N
A	L	S	D	I	F	U	H	I	M	M	I	N	E	N	T
L	B	X	Y	E	E	S	A	D	E	E	T	P	M	G	U
P	O	T	E	N	T	K	V	A	N	M	U	N	I	V	M
T	E	C	A	T	J	D	A	T	T	V	T	Q	N	E	U
E	L	B	I	C	S	A	R	I	O	N	E	I	E	U	L
V	W	A	S	O	F	P	I	N	U	B	O	M	N	T	T
I	T	N	Q	R	I	Z	C	G	S	O	C	K	T	T	U
U	E	E	P	I	L	A	I	M	B	U	L	J	R	I	O
A	F	F	O	D	E	M	O	O	D	C	B	N	O	S	U
G	Z	U	Y	H	A	S	U	O	I	C	I	L	A	M	S
Y	I	L	O	A	T	H	S	O	M	E	M	G	A	L	N

1. thin ______________
2. advisable ______________
3. near ______________
4. distinguished ______________
5. powerful ______________
6. important ______________
7. frightening ______________
8. baneful ______________
9. cross ______________
10. poverty-stricken ______________
11. stormy ______________
12. questioning ______________
13. greedy ______________
14. destined ______________
15. detestable ______________
16. cowardly ______________
17. agonizing ______________
18. wicked ______________

Name ______________________

Antonym Alias

Antonyms are words that have opposite meanings. For example *large* is an antonym for *small, broad* is an antonym for *narrow,* and *kind* is an antonym for *cruel.*

Because their names have become all too familiar to local police, each of the following criminals needs an alias. Create a nickname for each one by using an antonym for the first part of the name and then adding a name that begins with the same sound. You may use a dictionary to help you.

Example: Gregarious Gary = Reclusive Ron

1. Hardy Henry ______________________
2. Irksome Inez ______________________
3. Meticulous Mary ______________________
4. Ruthless Ricky ______________________
5. Suave Sam ______________________
6. Loathsome Larry ______________________
7. Precocious Pete ______________________
8. Genteel Gina ______________________
9. Expedient Ernie ______________________
10. Craven Chris ______________________
11. Clandestine Cathy ______________________
12. Bellicose Barb ______________________
13. Astute Annie ______________________
14. Garrulous Gavin ______________________
15. Antiquated Arnold ______________________

Name ______________________________

Take a Closer Look

The **denotation** of a word is its dictionary definition. The **connotation** of a word is another meaning it suggests or the shading given its dictionary definition by experience or association. For example, the **denotation** of the word *house* is a "dwelling or residence." The denotation of the word *mansion* is "a large dwelling or residence." According to the denotation, the primary difference is size; but experience and association have taught us that *mansion* connotes wealth and luxury, as well as larger size.

The connotations of words help to determine the impact they have on us. People who write advertisements select the words they use carefully. They are mindful of both the denotations and the connotations these words carry.

The following advertisement is filled with words that suggest, or connote, other meanings. As you read the ad, look for these words.

Looking for a Change?

We may have the answer. I-Spy Academy is offering a six-month course for would-be sleuths. If you are a clever, rugged, resourceful individual who is bored with routine, espionage may be for you. Imagine the excitement of learning to infiltrate enemy headquarters, hatch cunning plots, and decipher difficult codes. By the end of our low-priced program, you will be able to anticipate trouble before it happens and to defend yourself and others. Never again will you be a hapless victim. To register call 870-4143 today!

On the lines below, list words used in the ad that suggest other meanings to you. Beside each word write its denotation and its connotation.

	Word	Denotation	Connotation
1.			
2.			
3.			
4.			
5.			
6.			
7.			

Name ______________________________

Recognizable Relationships

An **analogy** is a relationship or correspondence between one pair of terms that serves as a basis for the creation of another pair. The terms in the second pair have the same relationship to each other as did the terms in the first pair. Some possible relationships are:

1. One word is an **antonym** of the other.
   Example: Old is to young as tall is to short.
2. One word is a **kind** of the other.
   Example: Bicycle is to vehicle as cat is to animal.
3. One word is a **part** of the other.
   Example: Toe is to foot as finger is to hand.
4. One word is a **synonym** for the other.
   Example: Big is to large as tiny is to small.

Sergeant Sloane is completing a refresher course in investigative techniques. Help him detect the relationship between the first two underlined words in each sentence below. Then circle the word in the columns to the right that is in similar relationship to the third underlined word.

1. Fugitive is to justice as runaway is to	plane	home	hate
2. Detect is to notice as hide is to	conceal	show	fur
3. Message is to code as face is to	eyes	smile	mask
4. Trigger is to gun as knob is to	hand	open	door
5. Clue is to solution as part is to	mechanic	whole	answer
6. Poverty is to wealth as young is to	ancient	new	mediocre
7. Policeman is to criminal as trapper is to	trap	rabbit	woods
8. Money is to bank as milk is to	cow	pitcher	drink
9. Winter is to season as December is to	month	Christmas	day
10. Verdict is to trial as diploma is to	education	students	marks

Name ____________________

Prove Your Case

To be a mystery, a story must have a crime, clues, excitement, suspense, and detection. Prove that a book you have read is a mystery by writing at least one paragraph in which you relate each of these qualities and characteristics to the book and cite specific examples.

A Crime: ____________________

____

____

____

____

Clues: ____________________

____

____

____

Excitement: ____________________

____

____

____

Suspense: ____________________

____

____

____

Detection: ____________________

____

____

____

For additional credit, choose and complete one of the following book projects: (1) Design a dust jacket for your book. (2) Draw a picture of your book's setting. (3) Create an ad to sell your book to someone else. (4) Pretend that your book has been made into a motion picture and make a movie poster for it. (5) Design your own project, have your teacher approve it, then do it.

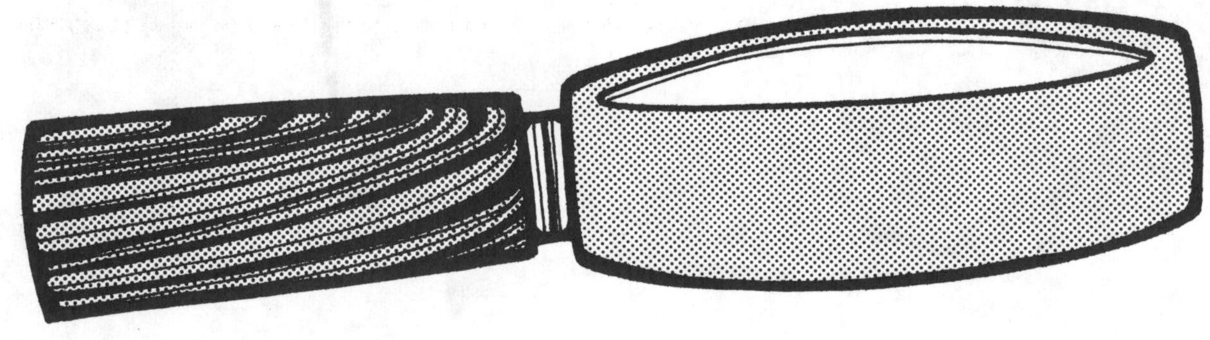

Name ____________________

Attention, All Mystery Buffs

To find the guilty party in the next murder mystery you read, just complete the chart below. The character with a motive, an opportunity, and a shaky alibi may well be the culprit.

Suspect	Motive	Opportunity	Alibi

Name ______________________________

Detective or Horror Story?

There are definite differences between detective stories and horror stories. Do you know how to tell them apart? Edgar Allan Poe wrote stories of both kinds and offered criteria for classifying them.

Edgar Allan Poe's Criteria

Detective Stories

1. are based on analysis and rational deduction.
2. reach a solution by means of a step-by-step recreation of the crime.
3. focus the reader's attention *not* on the crime or the suspects in the case, but on *how* the crime was committed.

Horror Stories

1. deal with mood and atmosphere rather than with characters and plot.
2. describe a series of horrors, piled one upon another, and rush to a swift climax.
3. hold the reader in a state of suspense until the last moment.

Select and read a detective or horror story. Then measure it against Poe's criteria.

1. Was the book you read a detective story or a horror story?

____

2. On the lines below, discuss specific passages or events from the book that match Poe's criteria and are the bases for your classification of it.

   a. On what was the book based or with what did it deal?

   ____
   ____
   ____
   ____

   b. What steps or events led to the solution or climax?

   ____
   ____
   ____
   ____

   c. On what was the reader's attention focused during the story?

   ____
   ____
   ____
   ____

Name ____________________

Key Codes

Can you crack the codes below? In the first code, letters stand for other letters. In the second, numbers are substituted for letters. The key to both is to look for short words or for repeated letters or numbers that may stand for vowels or double consonants.

Code I

Riddle:

I Z C W   B T O N   Q R   R G A T W
__ __ __ T   __ __ __ __   O __   __ __ __ __ T

N Q   H Z Q V W V   D O S Q L ?
__ O   __ __ O __ T __   __ __ __ O __ ?

Answer:

P Q Q P D G G T D V !
__ O O __ __ __ __ __ __ __ !

Code Letters:	A	B	C	D	E	F	G	H	I	J	K	L	M	N	O	P	Q	R	S	T	U	V	W	X	Y	Z
Substituted Letters:	__	__	__	__	__	__	__	__	__	__	__	__	__	__	__	__	O	__	__	__	__	__	T	__	__	__

Code II

Riddle:

18 17 3 20   9 7 15 12   6 19   5 25 3 10 10 11 10   12 6
__ __ __ __   __ __ __ __   __ __   __ __ __ S S E S   __ __

Answer:

5 17 6 10 20 10   18 11 3 23 ?
__ __ __ S __ S   __ E __ __ ?

10 13 11 1 20 23 11 1 25 11 10 !
S __ E __ __ __ E __ __ E S !

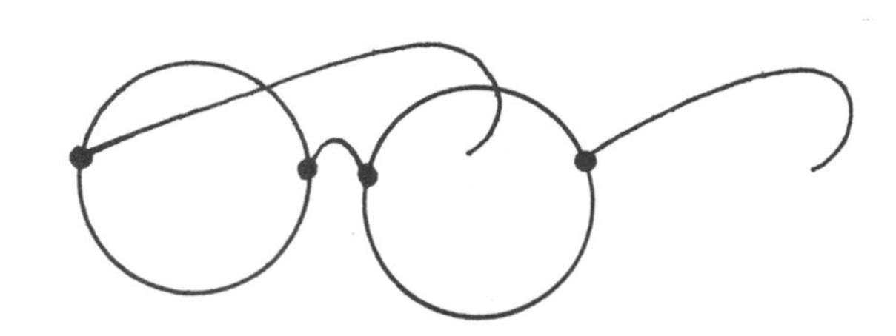

Code Numbers:	1	2	3	4	5	6	7	8	9	10	11	12	13	14	15	16	17	18	19	20	21	22	23	24	25	26
Substituted Letters:	__	__	__	__	__	__	__	__	__	S	E	__	__	__	__	__	__	__	__	__	__	__	__	__	__	__

T 17 C 8 D 3 1 Q 12 D T 15 4L 15 Q 10 D.

Name ____________________________

Punctuation Perfect

Imagine yourself in a bank shortly after a robbery has occurred. Because you are the sergeant in charge, you must interview the three persons who were in the bank when the crime took place. There is a small catch, however. Each of the three witnesses can respond only in the manner his or her name suggests. The names?

Sergeant Interrogator	yourself
Miss Exclaimer	the bank teller
Mr. Declarer	a customer
Mr. Imperative	the bank manager

Sergeant Interrogator: *Is there anyone here who can reconstruct the crime?*

Miss Exclaimer: ____________________________

____

Mr. Declarer: ____________________________

____

Mr. Imperative: ____________________________

____

Sergeant Interrogator: ____________________________

____

Mr. Imperative: ____________________________

____

Mr. Declarer: ____________________________

____

Sergeant Interrogator: ____________________________

____

Mr. Declarer: ____________________________

____

Miss Exclaimer: ____________________________

____

Check to make sure you have used the correct end punctuation. Then find three friends to take the parts of the bank teller, the customer, and the bank manager, and read your dialogue aloud with them.

Name ____________________

Sammy Suspense vs. Phony Phil

Sergeant Sammy Suspense has just received a note containing information that could lead to the arrest of Phony Phil, the counterfeiter Suspense has been pursuing for weeks. Unfortunately, many of the words in the note have been written in code. Can you help Sammy? Crack the scrambled-letter code and write the correct words on the lines below.

1. lrragyub ____________________
2. easc ____________________
3. uelsc ____________________
4. ricem ____________________
5. tolo ____________________
6. hopyn ____________________
7. wyntte-rollad ____________________
8. libls ____________________
9. eisfpgtrrnni ____________________
10. nchhu ____________________
11. llageli ____________________
12. vnsetgitiae ____________________
13. pescuts ____________________
14. diveeenc ____________________
15. liPh yonPh ____________________
16. negrrave ____________________
17. ipt ____________________
18. slatep ____________________
19. stemnabe ____________________
20. doog kluc ____________________

What did Sammy Suspense learn about Phony Phil? Using the words that you deciphered above, write the note you think Sergeant Suspense received on the lines below.

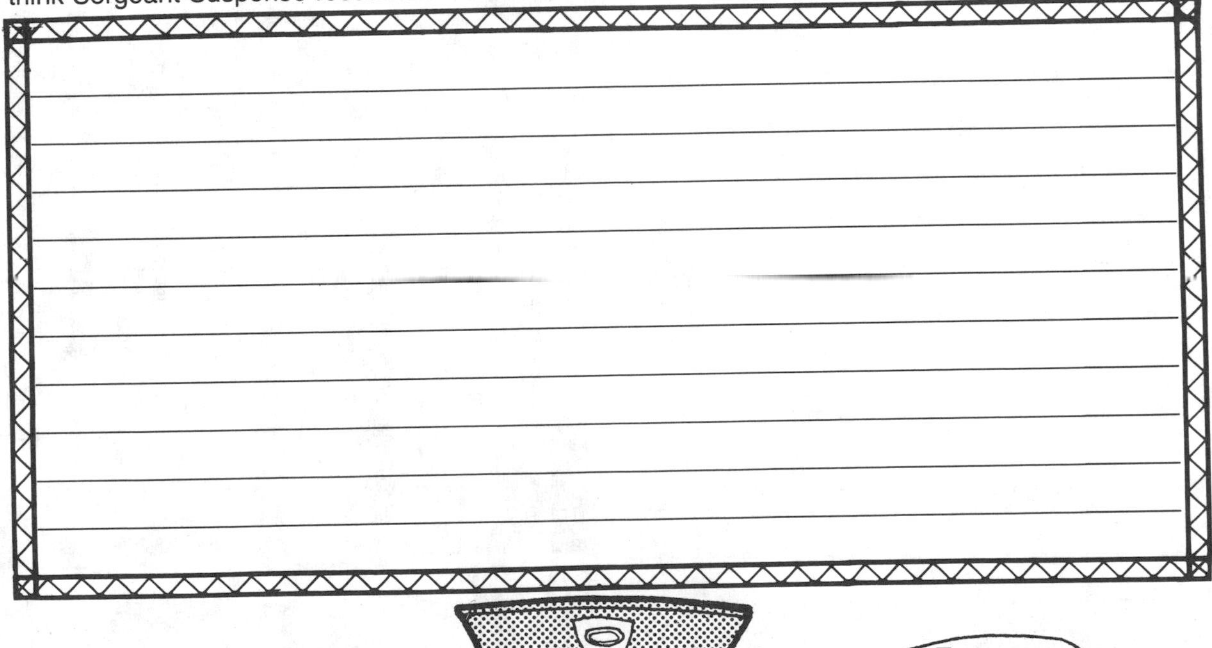

Name ______________________________

Mysterious Words

Using the letters in the boxes below, make as many words of two or more letters as you can. There's a catch, though. You can't use the letters at random. You can only use letters that are next to each other horizontally, vertically, or diagonally; however, you can use the same letter more than once. Write the words you make on the lines below.

M	Y	S
T	E	R
I	O	U
S		

1. ______________________________
2. ______________________________
3. ______________________________
4. ______________________________
5. ______________________________
6. ______________________________
7. ______________________________
8. ______________________________
9. ______________________________
10. ______________________________
11. ______________________________
12. ______________________________
13. ______________________________
14. ______________________________
15. ______________________________
16. ______________________________
17. ______________________________
18. ______________________________
19. ______________________________
20. ______________________________

Name ___________________________

Ghostly Words

1. Draw an outline of your favorite ghost or use the one on this page.
2. Cut out the ghost and cut two parallel horizontal slits each two inches long and about three-fourths inch apart across the ghost's midsection.
3. On a separate sheet of paper, list adjectives that could be used to describe a ghost or synonyms for a ghost. A dictionary or thesaurus may be helpful.
4. Cut a strip of paper a little less than two inches wide and as long as you need to write all of your words approximately one inch apart.
5. Copy your words onto the strip, spacing them approximately one inch apart.
6. Thread the top of the strip from the back of the ghost through the bottom slit, over the front of the ghost, and back through the top slit.
7. Adjust the strip so that the first word shows on top of the ghost.
8. Pull the strip slowly so that you can read the words.
9. Use your ghostly words to write a ghost story.
10. For some fresh word ideas, exchange ghosts with a friend.

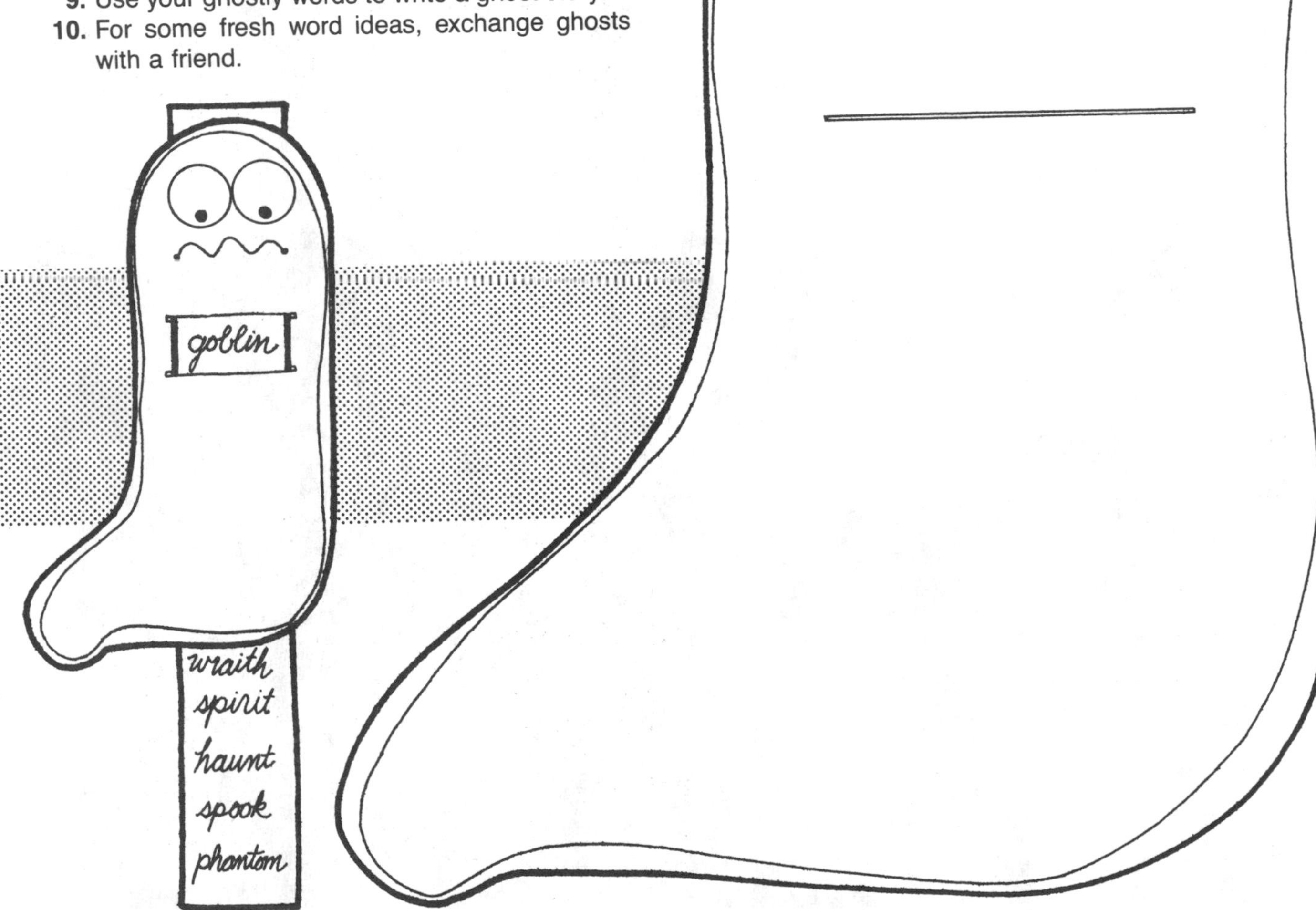

Name ______________________________

Pick a Partner—Produce a Play

Select a story that you have read this year to produce as a radio play. Then follow these steps.

1. Pick a partner—or two or three.
2. Reread the story together.
3. Make a list of the sound effects you will need.

Sound Effects

______________________	______________________
______________________	______________________
______________________	______________________
______________________	______________________

4. Make a list of the parts to be played.

Part	**To Be Played By**
______________________	______________________
______________________	______________________
______________________	______________________
______________________	______________________
______________________	______________________
______________________	______________________

5. Choose a narrator and assign the parts. Remember, in a radio play, one person can take several parts if he can change his voice so that listeners hear the difference.
6. Practice the play several times with sound effects.
7. Tape record your play.

Name ______________________________

What's in the Box?

You have just been handed a box. It is wrapped, taped, and padlocked. Prepare a pantomime in which you unwrap, untape, and unlock the box. Make clear to your audience what the mysterious box contains.

What's Behind the Door?

You have just come upon a secret door hidden behind the bookcases in an old library. Cautiously, you open the door. To your horror, you find . . .

Prepare a pantomime in which you discover the door, open it, and are horrified at what you see behind it. Or write a story in which you describe your horrifying experience.

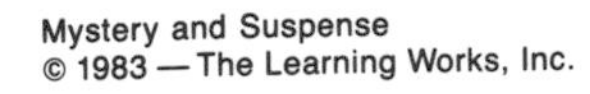

Name ______________________________

An Inside Job

You are Detective I. Spy. You have been assigned to investigate a robbery that has just occurred at a local bank. You soon discover that it was an inside job. Your suspects are:

Lisa Chatterbox, a secretary
Mr. Smirk, the bank teller
Mrs. Quick Swipe, the cleaning lady

Write at least ten lines of your dialogue with the suspects.

Name ____________________

Ghostly Game Board

Create a ghoulish game of your own using this Ghostly Game Board.

On a separate sheet of paper, write the rules for your game.

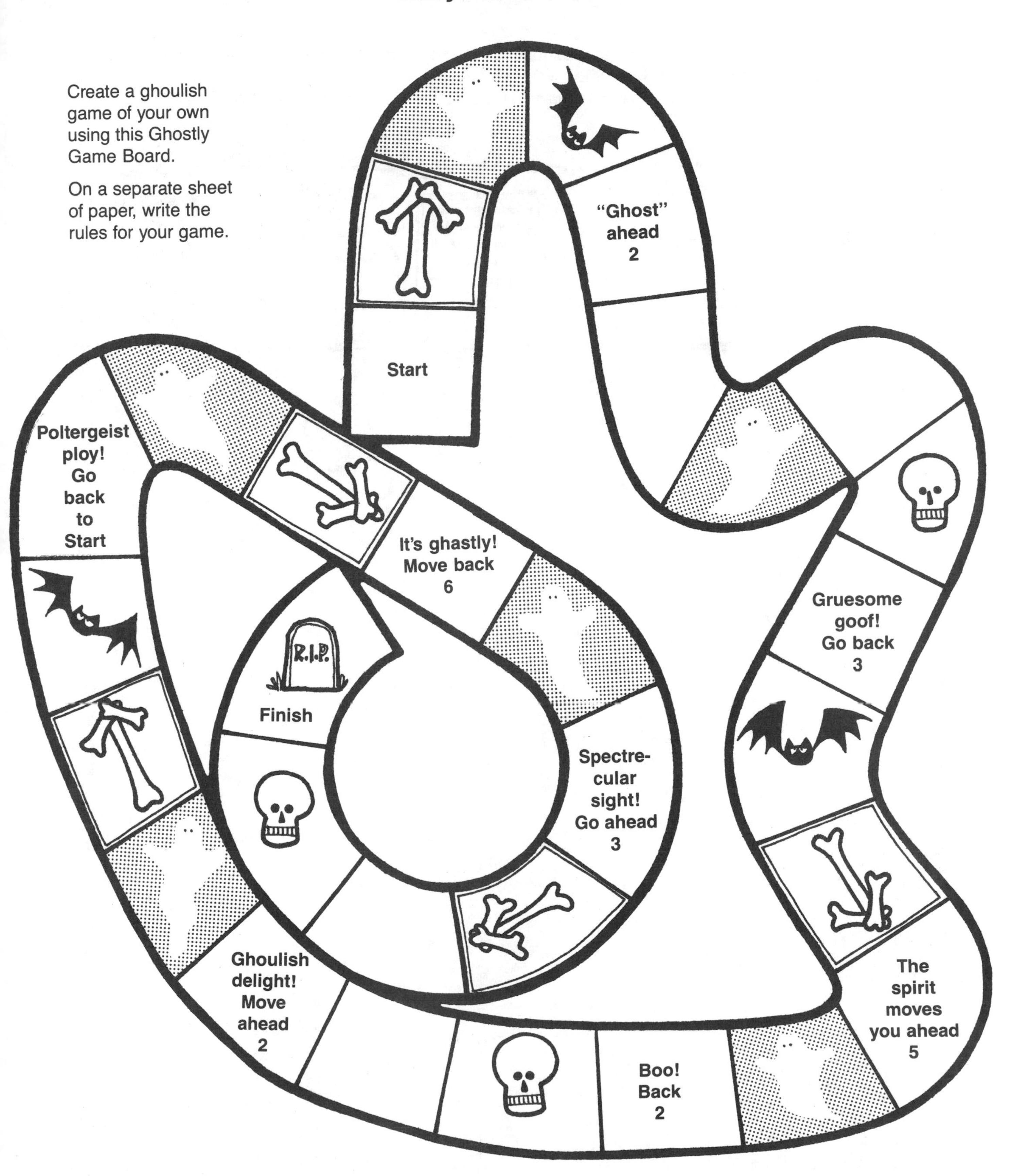

Name ______________________________

Secret Message

You are a secret agent. You need to pass accurate information about top secret documents along to your partner; but you are being watched closely. You want to disguise your message as a precaution in case it falls into the wrong hands, so you decide to use rebus writing. Read the sample below. Then write your note in the space provided.

Name ______________________________

Code Wheels

You don't have to continue using the same old code. Instead, you and a partner can make matching code wheels to use when you encode and decode messages. Then you can change codes as often as you like.

To make a code wheel, follow these simple steps.

1. Cut out the circles on page 90.
2. Glue the circles to tagboard or five-by-eight inch index cards.
3. Cut around each circle.
4. In the sections of the smaller circle, write letters, numbers, or symbols.
5. Punch a hole in the center of each circle.
6. Place the smaller circle on top of the larger circle and align the center holes.
7. Attach the two circles together by putting a brad through both center holes.

To use your code wheel, follow these steps.

1. Align a letter on the larger circle with any letter, number, or symbol on the smaller circle. For example, if you align the letter **A** on the larger circle with the letter **N** on the smaller circle, you are using the **A-N** code.
2. Encode your message, being careful to keep the sections of the two circles lined up.
3. Sign your name (in code, of course).
4. After your name, write the letter-letter, letter-number, or letter-symbol combination to indicate what code is being used. For example, in this instance you would write **A-N**.
5. Your partner can look at the letters following your name, align the circles on his or her code wheel as indicated, and decipher the message you have sent.

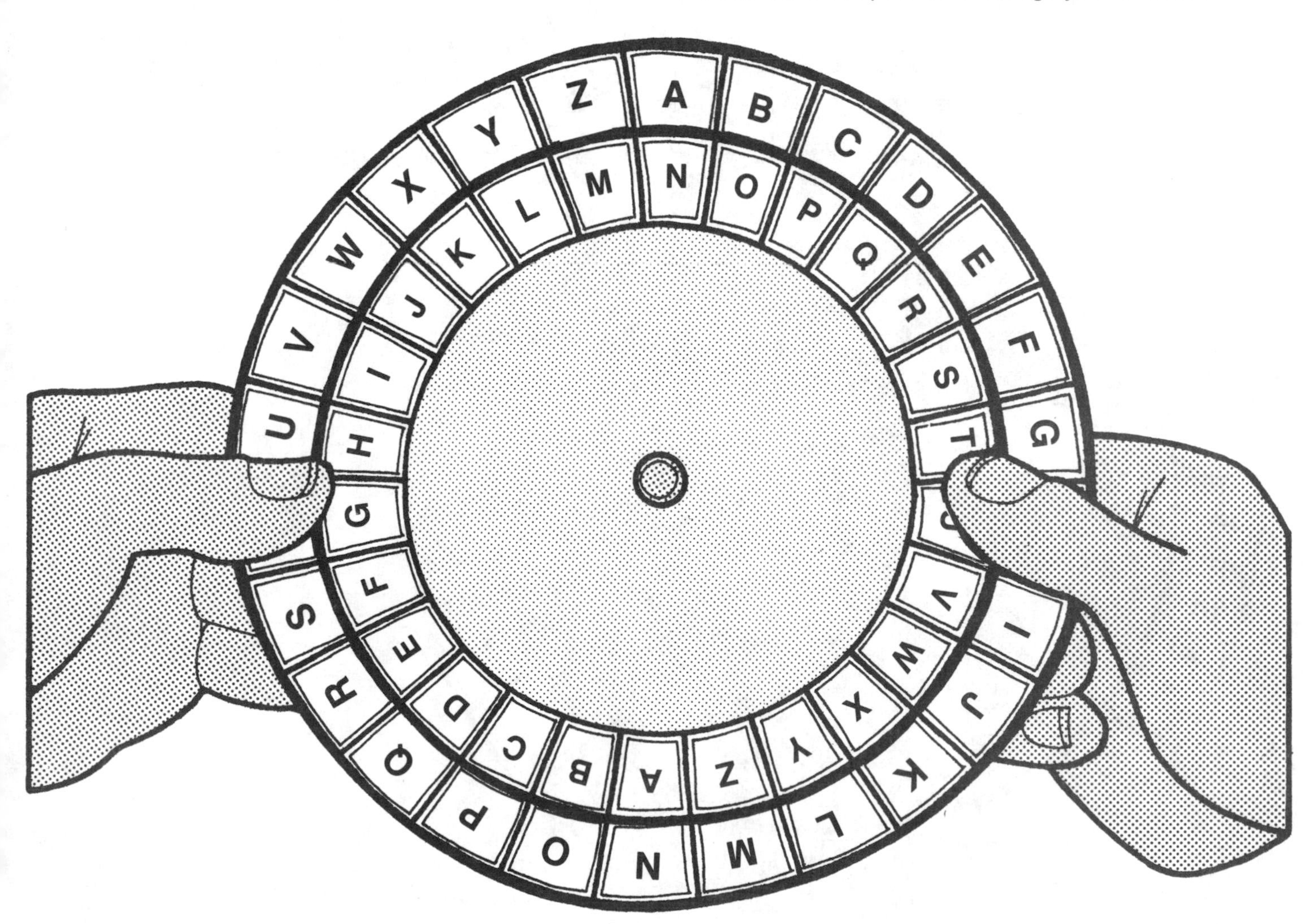

Name ____________________

Code Wheels
(continued)

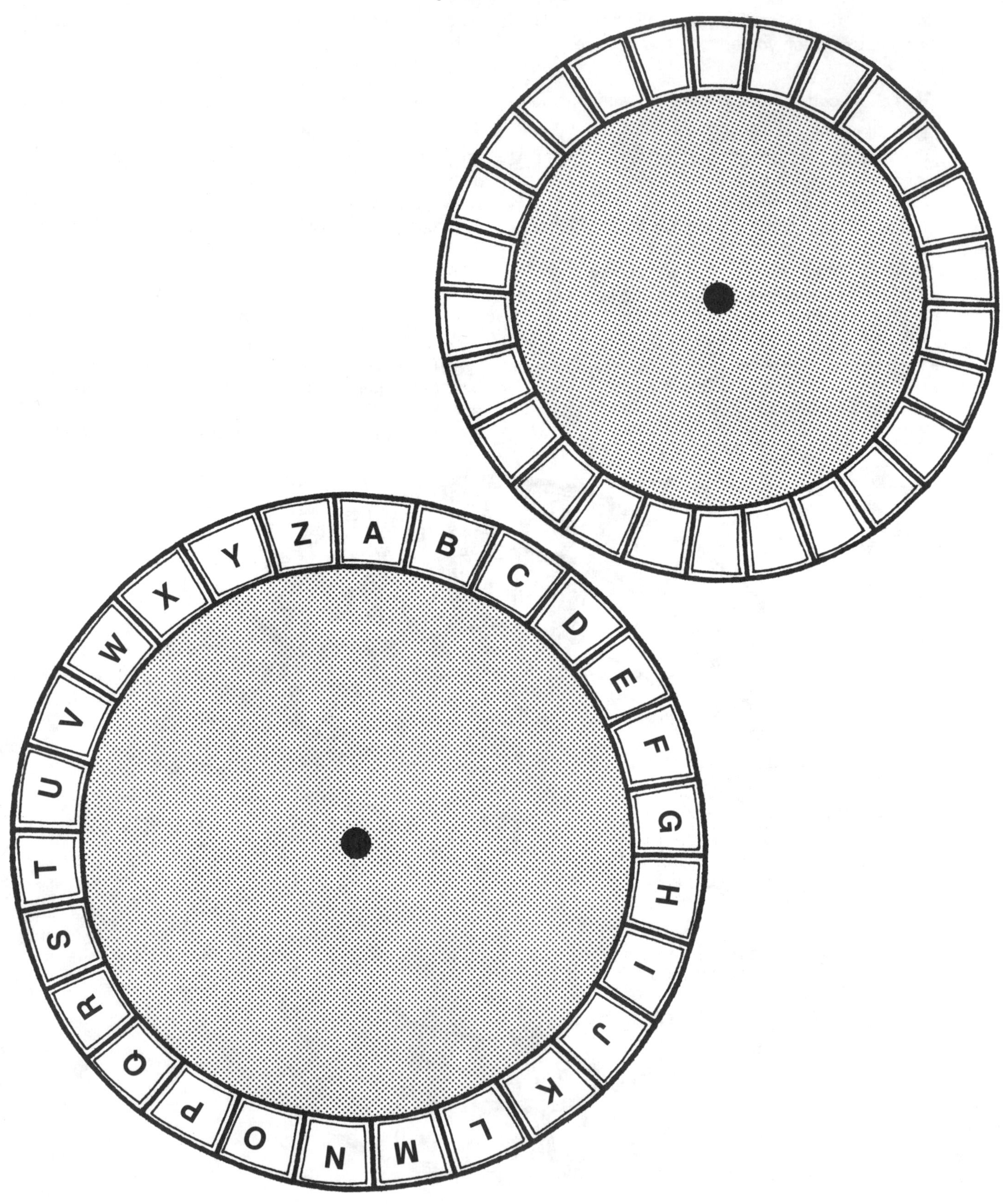

Name ______________________

The Baby-Sitting Burglary

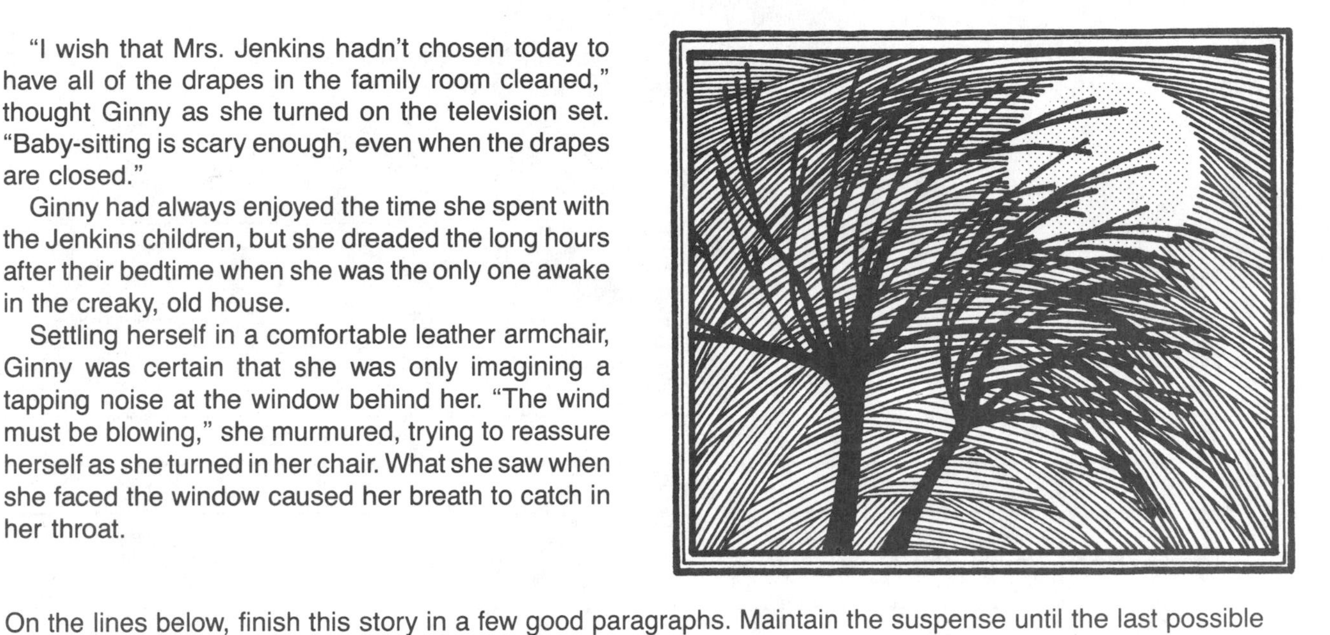

"I wish that Mrs. Jenkins hadn't chosen today to have all of the drapes in the family room cleaned," thought Ginny as she turned on the television set. "Baby-sitting is scary enough, even when the drapes are closed."

Ginny had always enjoyed the time she spent with the Jenkins children, but she dreaded the long hours after their bedtime when she was the only one awake in the creaky, old house.

Settling herself in a comfortable leather armchair, Ginny was certain that she was only imagining a tapping noise at the window behind her. "The wind must be blowing," she murmured, trying to reassure herself as she turned in her chair. What she saw when she faced the window caused her breath to catch in her throat.

On the lines below, finish this story in a few good paragraphs. Maintain the suspense until the last possible moment. Use an additional sheet of paper if you need it.

Name ________________________________

Trapped!

What would you do if you were locked in a museum with only three pennies, two pieces of bubble gum, a handkerchief, and a piece of string? On the lines below, write a letter to a friend telling of your plan for escape or rescue.

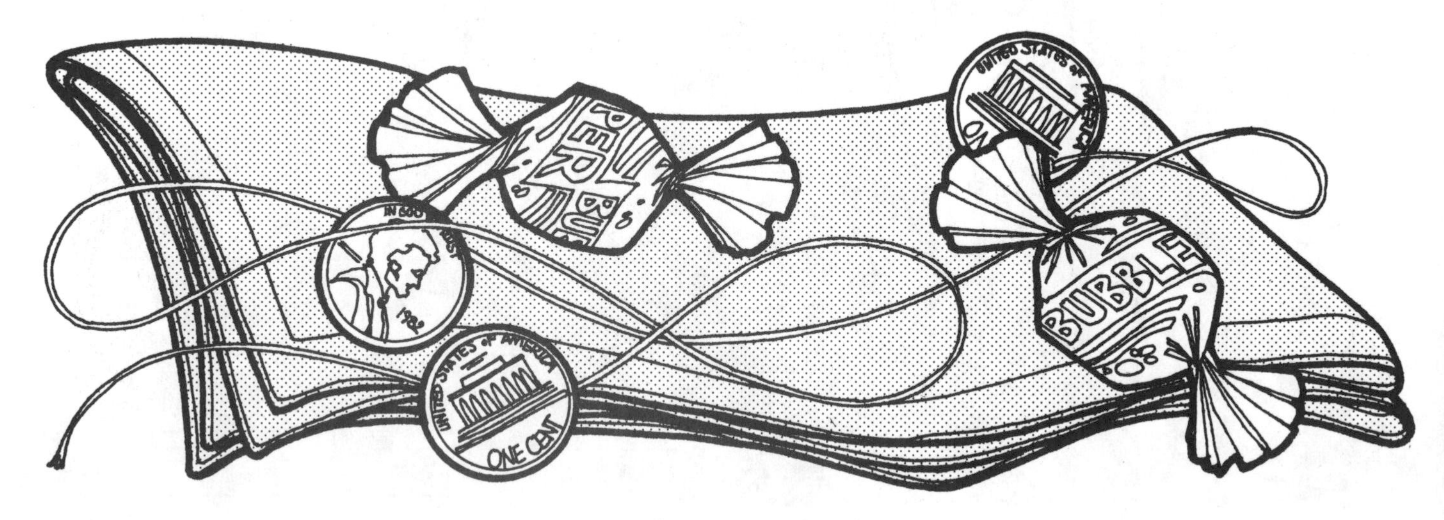

Name ____________________

Super Sounds

To create a library of Super Sounds that can be used in all kinds of radio dramas, follow these simple steps.

1. Choose a setting from those listed below and circle it.

   a beach on the ocean
   a Broadway theater
   a busy street in a big city
   a cave
   a dance studio
   a desert at night
   a fire station
   a forest
   a haunted house
   a hockey rink
   a jungle
   an office building
   a police station
   a schoolroom
   a subway station
   under water

2. On the lines below, list ten sound effects that would be appropriate for the setting you have chosen.

   ____________________ ____________________
   ____________________ ____________________
   ____________________ ____________________
   ____________________ ____________________
   ____________________ ____________________

3. Experiment to find ways to create these sounds. For example, rattling keys against a doorknob creates the sound of someone at a door; striking coconut shell halves together makes the sound of horses' hooves clomping along on a cobblestone or cement street.

4. When your sound effects are sufficiently realistic, tape record them. As you do so, leave a brief time interval between sounds.

5. List the sound effects you have recorded in order. Next to each, indicate where it can be found on the tape.

6. If you feel ambitious, choose another setting and tape record another series of sounds for your Super Sounds library.

Name ______________________________

Read at Your Own Risk

You have just visited the setting of one of your favorite mystery, suspense, or horror stories. On the lines below, write a letter to a friend describing your visit. Include details that will set your friend's spine tingling.

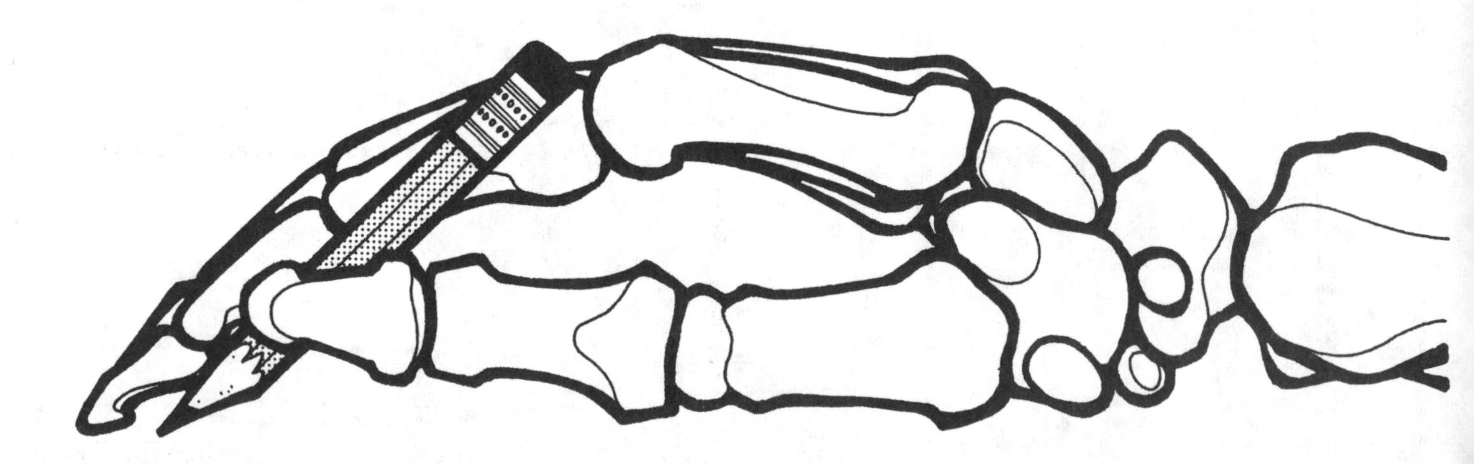

Name ______________________

Wordy Wonders

Can you unravel these expressions? Be careful! You will have to let your mind run in strange ways.

cover agent **she's an** 1. ______________	**dox** **dox** 2. ______________
ca se 3. ______________	**in** **her head** 4. ______________
Misplaced Body 5. ______________	**ecdoecodcode** 6. ______________
track a criminal 7. ______________	**man** **board** 8. ______________
go prison **prison** 9. ______________	**plagentace** 10. ______________

On a separate sheet of paper, make up five Wordy Wonders for a friend to figure out.

Name ________________________________

Combine the Clues

Your name is Detective Busbee. You have just been sent to the scene of a murder. You arrive to find that the corpse has disappeared. The only clues that remain are a partly eaten carrot, a gold coin, a golf club, a small bloodstain, and some blond hair. On the lines below, write a story in which you combine these clues to solve the crime. Use additional sheets of paper if you need them.

Name ____________________________

Puzzle Time

On the line beside each letter, write an adjective that starts with the letter and could be used to describe the word the letters spell.

S ____________________________
U ____________________________
S ____________________________
P ____________________________
E ____________________________
N ____________________________
S ____________________________
E ____________________________

On the lines below, create another mystery-and-suspense word puzzle for a friend to solve.

___ ____________________________
___ ____________________________
___ ____________________________
___ ____________________________
___ ____________________________
___ ____________________________
___ ____________________________
___ ____________________________
___ ____________________________
___ ____________________________

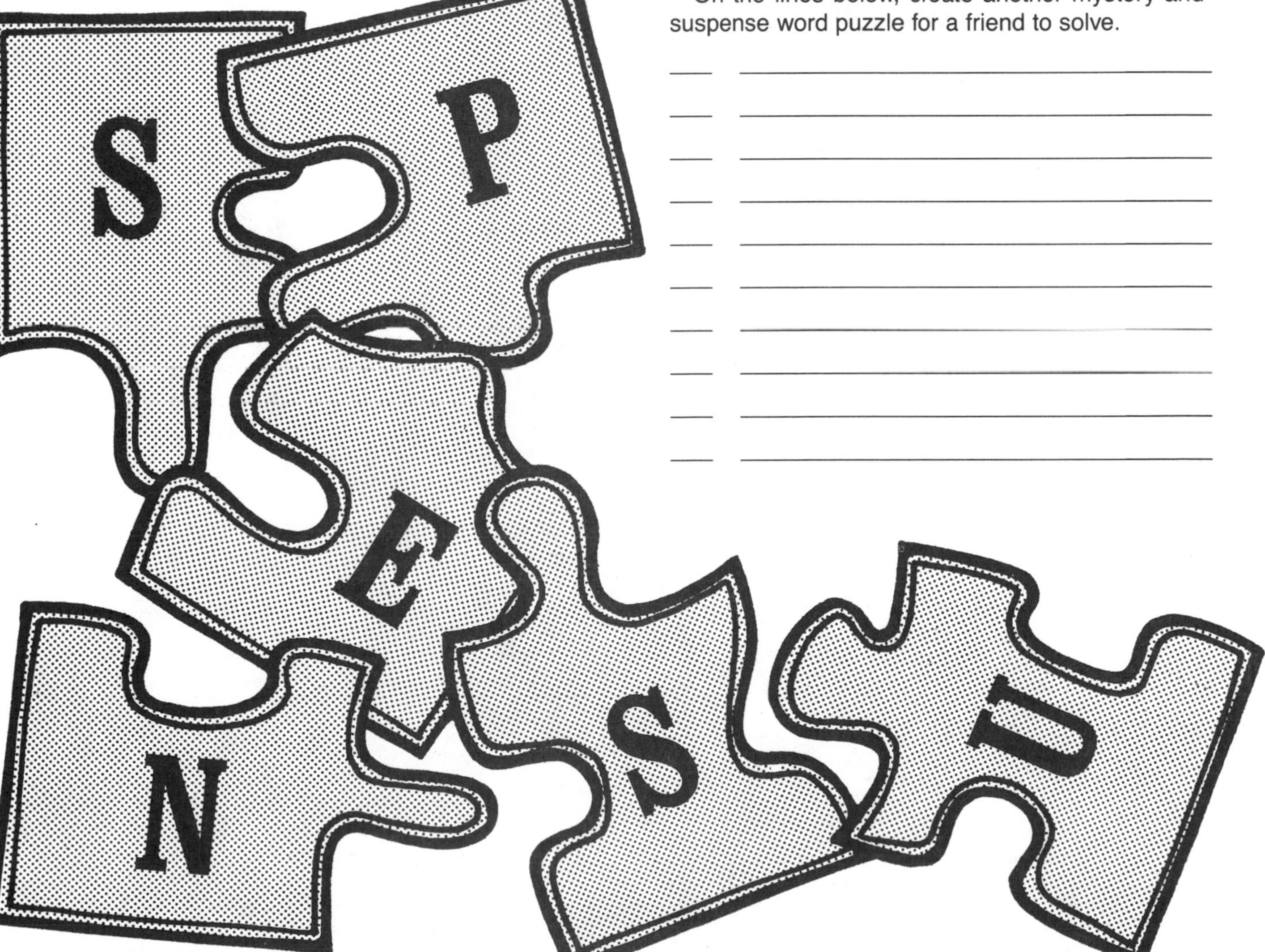

Name ____________________________

Take Care

Anyone who works as a secret agent knows how important it is to work undercover.

Imagine yourself as secret agent 213, assigned the job of rendezvousing in San Francisco with an agent whom you've never met. Fortunately, you've performed similar assignments before, so you're well aware of the importance of selecting an inconspicuous location and identifying yourself through seemingly innocent conversation.

On your last assignment, for example, you arranged a meeting in a Paris "jardin." You initiated the exchange with a comment on the beauty of the *flowers* in the park. To this, your contact replied "Yes, but to me there're nothing as beautiful as tall *sunflowers* swaying in a soft country breeze."

You smiled and completed the identification saying, "You must return to the park in the evening when all of the *flowers* are bathed in the light of the moon. It's even more beautiful then."

Convinced of your identity, he gave you the message he was carrying.

Now you try. Using the code words listed below, create five sets of code sentences that two agents might use to identify themselves and communicate a secret message.

camera
Chinese
menu
milkshake
newspaper
notebook
pen
pizza
streetlights
waitress

Is there any danger?
I was not followed.
Watch out!
I have the information.
I was followed.
Greeting for identification.
Reply for identification.
I have information but not here.
There is no danger.
The girl is the enemy.

____

____

____

____

____

____

____

____

____

____

____

____

Name ______________________________

Grave Messages

Although epitaphs are carved in tombstones, not all of them are grave messages. The epitaphs below were written with a light touch.

On a separate sheet of paper, design tombstones and write epitaphs for the following dear departed souls.

- Ebenezer Smith
- Ira Jones
- Abel Brown
- Zachariah Frim
- Sara Cheeves
- Charity Goodbrow

Name ______________________________

Haunted House

1. On the lines below, list ten words to describe this house.

   ______________________ ______________________
   ______________________ ______________________
   ______________________ ______________________
   ______________________ ______________________
   ______________________ ______________________

2. Who once lived in this house? ______________________________

   ____

3. Who haunts it now? ______________________________

   ____

4. Take your reader on a verbal tour of this haunted house. Be sure to include the ten descriptive words you listed above and lots of vivid verbs and adjectives. Use additional sheets of paper if you need them.

   ____

____
____
____
____
____
____

Name ____________________________

The Moneybag Mystery

Even though Detective I. C. Kloos was sitting in his office waiting for a telephone call, he was startled by the abrupt ring. Collecting himself, he reached for the receiver. "Hello, Detective Kloos here. What can I do for you? M-m-m, I see, m-m-m. 542 Bread Street. I'll be right there."

Kloos arrived at the address and rang the bell. When no one answered, he looked cautiously about, then slowly pushed open the door. A still form lay in the marble hallway. Upon closer examination, Kloos discovered it was Mr. I. Gotit, a well-known eccentric old millionaire. Gotit was alive but unconscious. Powdery footprints led from his side to a nearby closet. Kloos followed the footprints and carefully opened the closet door. Inside, Timothy Gopher, the butler, lay on the floor tied and taped. His frantic eyes looked appealingly up at Detective Kloos. Next to Gopher was a note. It said . . .

On the lines below, write the note you think Kloos found. Be sure to include other clues to the solution of the crime. Kloos will need them!

Individual Activity Sheet
Vocabulary

Name ______________________

Word Pictures

Select any six words from the list below. In the boxes, write each word you have selected in such a way that you illustrate its meaning.

capture	fear	puzzle
clever	guilty	scary
clue	horror	spiritual
dangerous	meek	terrifying
detect	protect	villain

Name ______________________________

The Pantomime Caper

You are Detective I. C. Kloos. You have just arrived at the scene of a crime. Prepare a pantomime in which you reveal (without speaking, of course) the crime that has been committed, the clues that have been left at the scene, and the identities of any witnesses who are available to answer your questions. On the lines below, make notes to help you in your pantomime caper.

1. Crime: ______________________________

2. Clues: ______________________________

____

____

____

3. Witnesses: ______________________________

____

____

____

____

____

Name ____________________

Super Sleuths

Choose a sleuth from the list below. Do research to learn what crime he or she solved. Then record the appropriate information on the Super Sleuth Scroll activity sheet on page 17 and share your findings with the class.

Detective Charles Chenivier, Paris, France
Detective Frank Falzon, San Francisco, California
Tuvia Freidman, Haifa, Israel
Detective Harry Hansen, Los Angeles, California
Tamegoro Igii, Tokyo, Japan
Dr. Friedrich Kuso, Vienna, Austria
Angelo Mangano, Rome, Italy
Sergeant John Murtough, Chicago, Illinois
James Mervyn Noble, Toronto, Canada
Milton Oliveira, Rio de Janeiro, Brazil
Superintendent Leonard Read of Scotland Yard, London, England

Real-Life Rogues

Choose a rogue from the list below. Do research to discover what crimes he or she was guilty of. Then record the appropriate information on the Real-Life Rogues activity sheet on page 16 and share your findings with the class.

Joe Adonis (Joseph Doto)
John Bellingham
Horatio Bottomley
John Wilkes Booth
Charles Buiteau
Al Capone
Frank Costello
Leon Czolgosz
Clarence Hatry
Bruno Hauptmann
Arthur and Nizamodeen Hosein
Ronald and Reginald Kray
Lord Kylsant
Nathan Leopold and Richard Loeb
Ferdinand Lesseps
Lee Harvey Oswald
Whitaker Wright

Mystery and Suspense Bibliography

Detective Stories

Adams, Samuel H.	"Aunt Minnie and the Accessory After the Fact"
Armstrong, Charlotte	"The Hedge Between"
Christie, Agatha	"The Dream"
Doyle, Arthur Conan	"The Hound of the Baskervilles"
	"Silver Blaze"
	"The Speckled Band"
Pentecost, Hugh	"The Day the Children Vanished"
Poe, Edgar Allan	"The Murders in the Rue Morgue"
Queen, Ellery	"Miser's Gold"
Rinehart, Mary Roberts	"The Splinter"
Sayers, Dorothy	"The Footsteps That Ran"
Stout, Rex	"The Gun with Wings"
Treat, Lawrence	"D as in Detail"
Wodehouse, P. G.	"Jeeves and the Stolen Venus"

The Mind of the Criminal

Allingham, Margery	"Bubblebath #3"
Brown, Margaret E.	"A Very Special Talent"
Harvey, W. F.	"August Heat"
Poe, Edgar Allan	"The Black Cat"
	"The Telltale Heart"

Horror and Imagination

Bangs, John Kendrick	"The Water Ghost of Harrowby Hall"
Bradbury, Ray	"The Veldt"
Brooke, Rupert	"Lithuania"
Collins, Wilkie	"A Terribly Strange Bed"
Fletcher, Lucille	"The Hitchhiker"
Jackson, Shirley	"The Whole Town Is Sleeping"
Jacobs, W. W.	"The Monkey's Paw"
Keller, David H.	"The Thing in the Cellar"
Matheson, Richard	"Duel"
Orczy, Baroness	"The Mysterious Death on the Underground Railway"
Poe, Edgar Allan	"The Pit and the Pendulum"
Saki	"The Open Window"

Reading Skills Checklist

List students' names on the lines at the left. When a skill is introduced, draw a diagonal line through the corresponding box and shade the upper portion. When that same skill is mastered, shade the remaining portion of the box.

	Vocabulary										Literal Comprehension							Interpretive Comprehension						Literary Terms											
Names	Analogies	Antonyms	Connotation/Denotation	Context Clues	Dictionary Skills	Multiple Meanings	Prefixes	Suffixes	Synonyms	Thesaurus	Comparison/Contrast	Fact or Opinion	Locating Information	Main Idea	Recognizing Author's Purpose	Sequencing	Supporting Details		Cause and Effect	Drawing Conclusions	Making Inferences	Point of View		Antagonist/Protagonist	Characterization	Climax	Conflict	Figurative Language	Flashback	Foreshadowing	Mood	Plot	Setting	Symbol	Tone

Name ______________________

Posttest

I. Match the terms on the left with the definitions on the right by writing the correct letter on each line.

____ **1.** plot
____ **2.** sequencing
____ **3.** foreshadowing
____ **4.** cause
____ **5.** effect
____ **6.** fact
____ **7.** opinion
____ **8.** compare
____ **9.** contrast
____ **10.** drawing conclusions
____ **11.** inference
____ **12.** climax
____ **13.** protagonist
____ **14.** antagonist
____ **15.** conflict
____ **16.** flashback
____ **17.** author's purpose
____ **18.** point of view
____ **19.** tone
____ **20.** setting
____ **21.** verbal imagery
____ **22.** mood
____ **23.** figurative language
____ **24.** symbol
____ **25.** context clues

A. the feeling the author wishes to create for the reader
B. an object, person, place, or event that can be used to stand for, represent, or suggest something else because of traditional association, emotional content, or accidental resemblance
C. a statement that has been or can be proved to be true
D. the leading character or hero of a story
E. the style or manner of expression, which reflects the author's attitude toward the material
F. the intent of the person who is writing
G. to show the ways in which unlike things are different
H. the sequence of events in a story
I. the time and place in which an event occurs
J. the turning point, the moment in which the conflict is resolved
K. to show the ways in which two similar things are alike or different
L. giving an indication or warning of what is to come so that the reader can anticipate the mood or action
M. language that is used creatively and imaginatively to evoke vivid images and to give fresh insights
N. the voice used to tell the story
O. a statement that is believed but cannot be proved
P. putting events in chronological order
Q. reaching a decision or making a judgment based on a body of evidence or group of facts
R. a struggle
S. what happened as a result of something
T. an opponent or adversary of the hero in a story
U. the reason for what happened
V. an educated guess based on facts or premises
W. an interruption in a story to permit the author to relate an event from the past
X. vivid figurative language used to create a clear word picture
Z. familiar words that help the reader determine the meanings of other, unfamiliar words

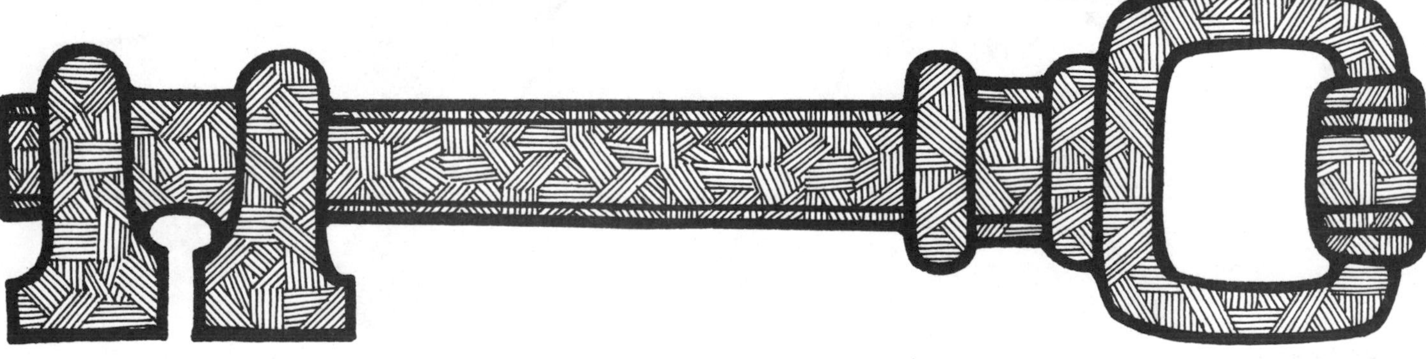

Name ______________________________

Posttest
(continued)

II. Read each question below. Then write the correct answer on the numbered line.

1. Complete the following **analogy**:

   Hero is to villain as hot is to — 1. ______________________________

2. Write a **synonym** for calm. — 2. ______________________________

3. Write an **antonym** for capture. — 3. ______________________________

4. "The judge told him he'd do a nice long stretch." Which meaning for the underlined word fits best in this sentence?

   distance   elongate   prison term — 4. ______________________________

5. What is one meaning of the **suffix** -er? — 5. ______________________________

6. In the word disapprove, what is the meaning of the **prefix**? — 6. ______________________________

7. Add a base word to the **suffix** -ful. — 7. ______________________________

8. In which book would you find more **synonyms** for a word, a thesaurus or a dictionary? — 8. ______________________________

9. The **connotation** of a word is the _______ that one attaches to it as a result of experience or association. — 9. ______________________________

10. Which one of the four kinds of **context clues** is given in the following sentence?

    The banker's wife was often bored, but the huge pile of gold intrigued her. — 10. ______________________________

Answer Key

Pages 7-9, Pretest

1. Lindsey
2. third person omniscient
3. outside a prison on a sunny day
4. Lindsey became a literacy volunteer.
5. The warden raced toward Lindsey.
6. "Funny how it had all seemed so different to her three months ago."
7. defeat; discouragement; exasperation; frustration
8. situation
9. resigned, trudged, sighing, loomed
10. man versus man and/or man versus society
11. "She turned and was amazed to see him [the warden] racing toward her."
12. Both were sunny.
13. On both Lindsey worked as a literacy volunteer.
14. Her mood has changed from optimistic to pessimistic.
15. She was unaware but has become aware of the obstacles she faces.
16. "like animal cages encased in cement"
17. Her smug assurance that she could make a difference.
18. fact
19. his belief that no one would hire him because he is a "jailbird"
20. Her efforts to help Jake seemed futile.
21. what the character says
22. what the character thinks
23. what the author tells the reader
24. Answers will vary.
25. Answers will vary.
26. quill
27. *Synonym:* complete
28. *Antonym:* incomplete; haphazard
29. stupid
30. Answers will vary.
31. the study of ________
32. far
33. restatement
34. a large dwelling or residence
35. wealth and luxury, as well as large size

Page 10, A Bungled Burglary

1. Two burglars came in.
2. They crept down the hall.
3. They tried to open the bedroom door.
4. George yelled.
5. He leaped out of bed.
6. He went charging down the hall.
7. A burglar hit George on the head.
8. George told his wife to call the police.
9. George passed out.
10. The burglars left.
11. George regained consciousness.
12. George discussed the crime with his wife.
13. George passed out again.

Pages 11-12, Teamwork Detective

Miss Able murdered Miss Smythe. The motive was jealousy. The weapon was a palette knife.
Reasoning: Florence Floogle locked the front door at midnight. Mr. Ready argued with Miss Smythe at 1:30 a.m. and then left the apartment forty-five minutes later, at 2:15. He returned the following evening with wine and flowers, obviously unaware that Miss Smythe was dead. Miss Able, on the other hand, was in the building, was in love with Mr. Ready, and had quarreled repeatedly with Miss Smythe.

Page 15, Cut-up Caper

The three were masked and were carrying guns.
One robber was reported to be a tall, blond woman.
They bolted the door as they entered.
They ordered Ms. Rix, the teller, to turn over the cash.
They locked the teller and two customers in a storeroom.

Ms. Rix and the customers managed to free themselves.
They notified the police at 3:45.
No one saw the robbers leave the bank.
An out-of-state car had been seen parked nearby.
The strange car disappeared about the time of the robbery.

The stopped car was driven by an irate elderly woman.
She told police that she was on her way to visit a sick relative.
The woman reported that she had been "passed like she was standing still" by a car just like her own.
A car answering this description was found abandoned about three miles from the Massachusetts border.
A blond wig was found in the car.
The police are now looking for three men.

A large powerboat reported stolen from the New Haven Harbor may have been their escape vehicle.

Page 18, Find the Foreshadowing

I. The words "things are definitely looking up" foreshadow a change. Answers will vary.
II. seemed
III. Answers will vary.
IV. Answers will vary.

Page 19, Expect an Effect

I. 1. Hector had to find a place to hide because (the police were looking for him.)

2. He had robbed the bank because (he was desperate for money.)

3. Because (Hector had left fingerprints on the front door of the bank,) the police knew he was the criminal.

Page 19, Expect an Effect

4. They would be able to recognize him because he had forgotten to wear a disguise.
5. Because he was frightened, Hector made some stupid mistakes.
6. He ran to his home because he could not think of anywhere else to go.
7. The police were sure to check his home because they had it staked out.
8. Hector burned the money in the fireplace to destroy the evidence.
9. To remember the event, however, he kept one bill.
10. Because he was so foolish, the police were able to charge him with the crime.

Page 20, Expect an Effect (continued)

II. 1. E 2. B 3. A 4. D 5. C
III. 1. C 2. A 3. E 4. D 5. B

Sequence Review
1. John Meyers could not go to sleep.
2. He listened very carefully.
3. John looked out the window.
4. He turned on a flashlight.
5. John screamed.

Page 22, Factual Facts and Obvious Opinions

1. F 2. F 3. F 4. O 5. F 6. F 7. O 8. O 9. F
10. F 11. O 12. O 13. F 14. F 15. F

Page 23, Create a Crime

Answers will vary.

Page 25, Detail Detective

Differences
1. briefcase (*or* folder), dog tag, *or* necktie
2. In Picture A, the man has a full head of hair; in Picture B, he is almost bald.

Similarities
1. Both pictures show a man grudgingly giving paper (possibly money) to a boy (*or* youth).
2. Both pictures contain a man, a boy, and a dog.

Contrast
1. The boy's brow is unfurrowed, while the man's brow is deeply lined in a frown.
2. The boy's mouth is open pleasantly, possibly in a smile, while the man's mouth is formed to scold or yell.

Page 26, Proctor City Problem

Pat the Policemen: cold, emotional, honest, male, middle-aged, neat, patient, power-hungry, short-tempered, single, stubborn, thorough, trustworthy

Tony the Thug: cold, dangerous, dishonest, emotional, greedy, male, neat, patient, power-hungry, short-tempered, single, stubborn, thorough, young

Contrast sentences will vary.

Pages 27-29, Tune in Tomorrow

Episode One
1. The murder apparently took place in a hospital.
2. Clues—white coat, intercom, thin-handled knife

Episode Two
1. You know that Sally feels guilty about something because she is described as *creeping* into the room and looking *nervously* about. The fact that she waited before screaming indicates that she knew the corpse was there.
2. You should remember that Sally is right-handed.

Episode Three
1. The doctor's observation and the now-stiffening hand.
2. The crime was committed in the early evening, shortly before the dinner hour.

Episode Four
1. Small knows more than he's admitting. He refers to stabbing when he has not yet seen the body and immediately associates the scrap of paper with Jim's death when he has been given no reason to do so.
2. Tables running the length of the room and the notation on the scrap of paper suggest that the murder scene is some kind of laboratory.

Episode Five
1. Sawyer and Small are probably in collusion. You can make this assumption because they both worked with Jim Seward before his untimely death.
2. The crime took place in the laboratory of a company that produces fibers. You know from clues given previously and from mention of "the fiber."
3. You can now assume that Small committed the murder. The placement of the knife indicates that the stabbing was done by a left-handed person, and Small is left-handed. (Sally, you will remember, is right-handed.)
4. The determined gentleman with Sally Sawyer is probably the owner of the company and/or the director of the laboratory.

Page 30, Caption This

1. The damsel is screaming because a man has grabbed her arm, and she is frightened.
2. The villain is smiling because he has overpowered the damsel and is about to grab her necklace.
3. The damsel looks angry (*or* determined) and is clearly about to strike her attacker.
4. The villain has been knocked out, and the story ends happily.

Page 34, Inference Incidents

Answers will vary.

Page 36, Quick Crimes

1. Bartlett revealed information that he could not have known if he was innocent.
2. Bartlett said he had warned his wife not to drive herself home if she had been drinking. Then he made specific reference to the "bad stretch of road."

Page 46, Cases in Conflict

1. Man versus Himself
2. Man versus Nature
3. Man versus Society
4. Man versus Man

Page 48, Focus on Flashback

I. *Chronological Order:* 3, 10, 1, 8, 2, 6, 7, 5, 9, 4
Narrative Order: E, J, C, A, D, H, I, G, B, F

II. The underlined words should be "let his mind wander back to the events that had led to his current predicament."

Page 49, What's the Purpose

I. to inform
II. to persuade
III. to entertain

Page 51, The Tone at the Time Is . . .

1. The author is addressing fellow citizens of a town (*or* the readers of a newspaper) through its editorial column.
2. He or she expresses contempt for Bill Able.
3. He or she expresses disgust with the juvenile justice system.
4. The tone of the editorial is angry.

Page 52, Setting Sampler

I. 1. The scene takes place in the evening. The words, "their faces reflected in the illuminated shop windows," tell you so.
2. The scene takes place on the main street of some town. The words, "headed down Main Street," tell you so.
3. The next scene will take place at the Sand Pit. This setting will be very important because it is where the "showdown," or confrontation, will take place.

II. 1. The story takes place in the late 1800s or early 1900s.
Circled words—*riverboat, beribboned girls, knicker-clad boys*
2. The story takes place in the South.
Underlined words—*bundles of cotton*

III. 1. The story takes place in the 1960s.
2. The specific location probably will be important to the story. The author describes this setting in detail—expectancy before a rock concert; large numbers of adults, children, and animals; nervous officials outside a fenced area; chaos and confusion.

Page 53, Verbal Imagery

Answers will vary.

Page 55, Create-a-Story Worksheet

Answers will vary.

Pages 56-57, Mood Messages

I. Answers will vary.

II. 1. Sara is walking quickly on pavement past deserted storefronts and narrow alleyways.
2. Sara finds herself being shot at by someone.
3. The mood is one of suspense and fear.

III. 1. John's mood is expressed in the words: "He had known all along that it would be a disaster. For an unknown sixteen-year-old to defeat cyclists who were so much more experienced simply was not possible."
2. The author's only description of the setting is in the words, "The road stretched unendingly before him."
3. The words "colored" by John's frame of mind are *throbbing, unendingly, far distance,* and *smug forms.*

Page 58, Mood Magic

Answers will vary.

Page 59, Figuratively Speaking

1. a. A siren sounded.
b. Machine-gun fire was heard.
c. People ran and dodged.
d. Lights flashed.
e. The noise and motion stopped.
f. The border was quiet again.

2. a. a shrill, screech- or scream-like sound
b. the short, clear-cut, rhythmic, and unconnected sound of automatic weapon fire
c. shooting ammunition
d. The image likens fleeing people to crabs that, when startled, scurry from the sunlight into the sheltering darkness of an overhanging rock at the water's edge.
e. The word *scuttle,* meaning both "a short, swift run" and "a hurried withdrawal from occupied territory," reinforces the crab image. The people described in the story run quickly for short distances and then duck behind something or into the darkness to avoid being shot.
f. The inanimate barbed wire is likened to an octopus that reaches out and grabs. In truth, of course, the clothing of the fleeing victims is caught on the barbed wire as they run past it.
g. making an irregular pattern against the dark sky
h. The noise and motion stopped.

3. Answers will vary.
4. Answers will vary.

Page 61, The Context Connection

1. 4, continually, without stopping
2. 2, vengeance
3. 1, spying
4. 4, opposite
5. 4, approve, condone
6. 4, homeless wanderer with no apparent source of income

Page 64, Eye Spy Suffixes

-less: dauntless, guileless, helpless, hopeless, useless
-ous: adventurous, murderous
-ful: beautiful, hopeful, useful
-er: camper, employer, helper, jeweler, murderer, searcher

Page 65, Would You If You Could?

1. yes 2. yes 3. no 4. no 5. no
6. no 7. no 8. no 9. yes 10. yes

Page 67, Target Practice

1. timorous	11. momentous
2. potent	12. malicious
3. doomed	13. intimidating
4. avaricious	14. discerning
5. expedient	15. destitute
6. quizzical	16. loathsome
7. eminent	17. emaciated
8. tumultuous	18. imminent
9. excruciating	19. apprehensive
10. pernicious	20. irascible

Page 70, Try the Thesaurus
Answers will vary.

Page 71, Get in the Synonym Spirit

1. avarice	greed
2. blame	accuse
3. culpable	guilty
4. aid	abet
5. abhor	detest
6. criminal	felon
7. acquit	release
8. reconnaissance	surveillance
9. compensation	redress
10. larceny	robbery
11. vindictive	vengeful
12. spite	malice
13. ghastly	grisly

Page 72, Double Trouble

1. thin	emaciated
2. advisable	expedient
3. near	imminent
4. distinguished	eminent
5. powerful	potent
6. important	momentous
7. frightening	intimidating
8. baneful	pernicious
9. cross	irascible
10. poverty-stricken	destitute
11. stormy	tumultuous
12. questioning	quizzical
13. greedy	avaricious
14. destined	doomed
15. detestable	loathsome
16. cowardly	timorous
17. agonizing	excruciating
18. wicked	malicious

Page 73, Antonym Alias
Answers will vary.

Page 74, Take a Closer Look
Answers will vary.

Page 75, Recognizable Relationships

1. home	6. ancient
2. conceal	7. rabbit
3. mask	8. pitcher
4. door	9. month
5. whole	10. education

Page 79, Key Codes
Riddle: What kind of fruit do ghosts enjoy?
Answer: Booberries!
Riddle: What kind of glasses do ghosts wear?
Answer: Spectrecles!

Page 81, Sammy Suspense vs. Phony Phil

1. burglary	11. illegal
2. case	12. investigate
3. clues	13. suspect
4. crime	14. evidence
5. loot	15. Phony Phil
6. phony	16. engraver
7. twenty-dollar	17. tip
8. bills	18. plates
9. fingerprints	19. basement
10. hunch	20. good luck

Sample Note: While investigating a burglary case, I came across some clues to another crime. Among the loot we recovered were some phony twenty-dollar bills with fingerprints on them. I have a hunch something illegal is going on and suggest that you investigate. I suspect the evidence will point to Phony Phil, who was once an engraver. We have received a tip that the plates are hidden in his basement. Good luck!

Page 82, Mysterious Words
Answers will vary, but possible words include the following: item, me, met, my, mystery, route, ruse, serious, set, sit, site, sitter, so,sorry, system, terror, to, yes, yet, your.

Page 88, Secret Message
I'm sure you will see the light. Other answers will vary.

Page 95, Wordy Wonders
1. She's an undercover agent.
2. paradox
3. crack *or* break the case
4. in over her head
5. The Case of the Misplaced Body
6. mixed-up *or* scrambled code
7. track down a criminal
8. man overboard
9. go two (*or* to) prison
10. agent in place

Pages 107-108, Posttest

I. 1. H 2. P 3. L 4. U 5. S 6. C 7. O 8. K 9. G 10. Q 11. V 12. J 13. D 14. T 15. R 16. W 17. F 18. N 19. E 20. I 21. X 22. A 23. M 24. B 25. Z

II. 1. cold
2. gentle; tranquil; lull; quiet; still
3. discharge; emancipate; free; liberate; release
4. prison term
5. one who does
6. not
7. beautiful; careful; thoughtful
8. a thesaurus
9. meaning
10. contrast